BEST BY FAR
TWILIGHT OF THE GODS
BOOK ONE

Brittany Graves

Copyright © 2025 by Brittany Graves

All rights reserved.

No part of this publication may be reproduced, distributed, or transmitted in any form or by any means, including photocopying, recording, or other electronic or mechanical methods, without the prior written permission of the publisher, except as permitted by U.S. copyright law. For permission requests, contact the author at brittany.graves.books@outlook.com.

The story, all names, characters, and incidents portrayed in this production are fictitious. No identification with actual persons (living or deceased), places, buildings, and products is intended or should be inferred.

Book Cover by Amber Thoma.

First edition 2025.

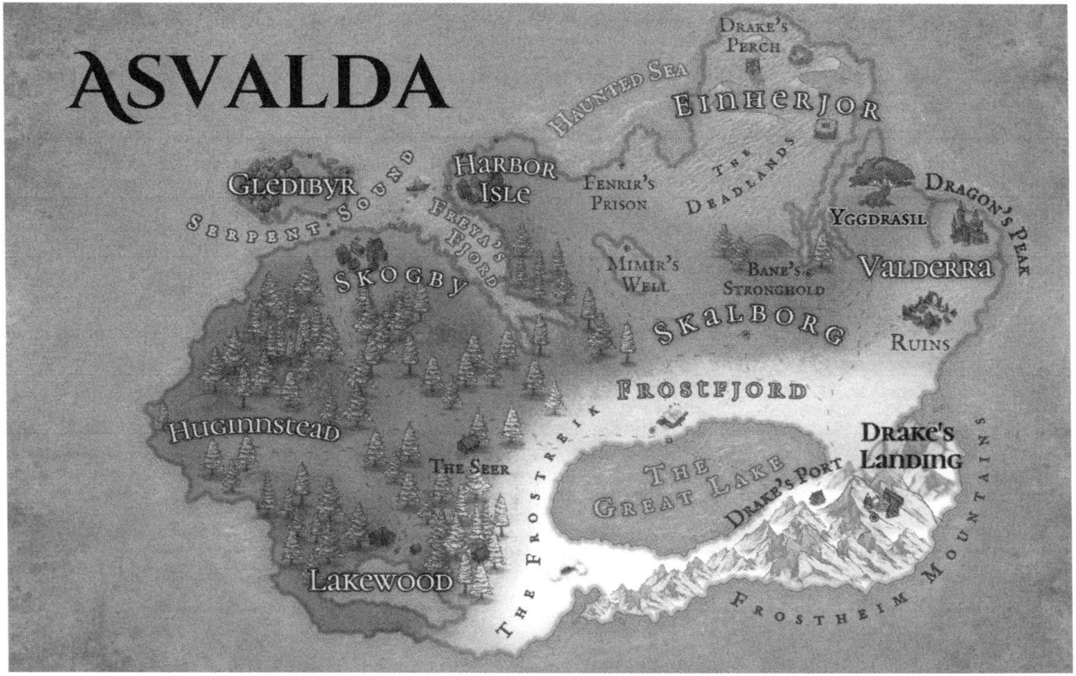
ASVALDA
Drake's Perch
Haunted Sea
Einherjor
Harbor Isle
Gledibyr
Serpent Sound
Freya's Fjord
Fenrir's Prison
The Deadlands
Yggdrasil
Dragon's Peak
Skogby
Mimir's Well
Bane's Stronghold
Valderra
Skalborg
Ruins
Frostfjord
Huginnstead
The Seer
The Great Lake
Drake's Port
Drake's Landing
The Frostreik
Lakewood
Frostheim Mountains

Table of Contents

Dedication	VII
Content Warning	VIII
Prologue	1
Chapter One	9
Chapter Two	18
Chapter Three	34
Chapter Four	46
Chapter Five	50
Chapter Six	62
Chapter Seven	68
Chapter Eight	77
Chapter Nine	83
Chapter Ten	91
Chapter Eleven	97
Chapter Twelve	107
Chapter Thirteen	111
Chapter Fourteen	120

Chapter Fifteen	130
Chapter Sixteen	134
Chapter Seventeen	142
Chapter Eighteen	149
Chapter Nineteen	157
Chapter Twenty	165
Chapter Twenty-One	174
Chapter Twenty-Two	182
Chapter Twenty-Three	194
Chapter Twenty-Four	198
Chapter Twenty-Five	204
Chapter Twenty-Six	208
Chapter Twenty-Seven	219
Chapter Twenty-Eight	224
Chapter Twenty-Nine	231
Chapter Thirty	232
Epilogue	243
Acknowledgements	247
About the author	249

To my beautiful daughter,
Arwen Jude.
You inspire me every single day,
and give me the purpose I have always needed.
I love you.

Content Warning

First, I am beyond excited for this book to be in your hands.

Best By Far is heavily inspired by the Norse Prophecy: Ragnarök. There have been many changes made to the folklore and mythology of the Nordic culture in order to fit this story, I want everyone to be aware that it is not exactly the same. So for my fellow Viking nerds, just hang in there—there are many Easter Eggs as well.

In Best By Far you can expect to find some themes that may not be suitable for everyone. There are some violent themes and difficult conversations between characters within this series, and it is important that I give everyone ample warning before jumping into the story.

Some possible triggering topics include: Death of a loved one, mentions of domestic abuse, PTSD, mentions of torture, death of children (not in scene, not main characters).

Knowing some of these topics can be very difficult, please feel free to reach out for specific areas where these themes occur, or just more details if necessary.

With that being said, I hope you enjoy the story, and thank you so much for reading!

Sincerely,

Brittany Graves

PROLOGUE

The Princess couldn't recall a time where she had ever seen her home anything less than perfect. In any instance of disarray, the castle thralls would immediately be put to work and ensure everything was pristine. As the most modern architectural masterpiece of the age, expectations for the castle's appearance and durability were of the utmost importance. Buildings have been made with stone for decades now, but nothing quite so vast as the home of Asvalda's Royal Family.

No, Dragon's Peak had never been anything less than perfect. So when there wasn't a person to be seen as the Princess ran through the halls of her home, thunder roaring with the summer winds, and terrified screams from the city below—she knew that would no longer be the case. Dragon's Peak would surely fall in whatever war was happening just beyond its walls.

When the Princess succumbed to the realization that she needed to find the King and Queen rather than looking for information from passerby, she quickly turned into a nearby thrall tunnel to get to the throne room in secret. She couldn't risk being seen in case enemies had already breached the castle. She was the only Asvaldan heir, and it had always been paramount that the Kingdom should never lack a ruling female in the royal bloodline.

The tunnels were mostly dark, only lit by the occasional brazier too close to the ceiling. As the Princess ran, the walls grew tight around her, as if they could swallow her whole. The soles of her slippers rapidly tore apart, not used for such rough terrain, only smooth stone floors and plush carpets. Dust clung to her sweat coated skin as she continued to run. Suddenly, she lost her footing and tumbled into the wall. Her breathing was labored and weighed by fear, confusion congested her thoughts.

Where was everyone?

Who was attacking the castle?

Why?

She eventually came to a fork in the tunnel, not plagued with the typical fear of getting lost, as she had each passageway memorized for this exact purpose–evacuation. The path to the left would lead her to the throne room, the middle would bring her further beneath the castle, to a direct route to safety. The path to the right…well there shouldn't be a path to the right.

Thinking back to all of the maps of the castle hideaways she has gone over; she has never seen this path before. Where could it possibly go?

So far, she heard nothing except for her heavy breathing, her slippers assaulting the gravel, and her heartbeat hammering in her ears. There certainly had been no sign of a soft harmony floating through the darkness until that moment, a soft ballad that no common bard could ever play so serenely. Yet this song emanated from the third path, and taunted the Princess with its magic. She could feel the pull on her own power, like a small rope tugging at her chest to obey.

The Princess had always been known for her practical nature. Certainly not one to choose a mysterious path; clearly born from a foreign magic. She recognized the possible trap in the decision to move forward but pushed the thought aside carelessly. The song promised her safety, it promised her a future. So rather than racing to the throne room to find her parents as taught, she followed the magic and simply hoped that wherever it would bring her, it was worth the cost.

The second she stepped into the new tunnel she felt as if she was floating off the ground. Her insides churned as she frantically searched her surroundings for an answer to what was making her feel such a way. When she glanced down at her body, her breathing hitched, and stomach dropped. She should have seen a satin nightgown and ruined slippers. Auburn hair should have been grazing her elbows, and pale freckled skin should have been glowing in the low light of the tunnel. Instead, she only saw the gravel floor beneath her missing feet. She had completely disappeared, but quickly realized she could still be heard as her single step forward echoed around her. Panic attempted to seize her–nearly succeeding–until she heard a small creature approaching from the mysterious path. Once the fiery glow from the closest brazier shimmered on velvet fur, it dawned on her that there was a rabbit in this darkness as well. An unlikely creature with an unlikely person to be in such a place.

It was covered in hazelnut fur and had round intelligent amber eyes to match the dim flames above. The Princess was in awe of her bravery to approach a human while nothing but destruction surrounded them all. The rabbit tilted her head, as if waiting for the Princess to recognize her.

"You are a beauty, little one, but what are you doing down here? How did you get in?" she asked quietly, her breathing having slowed significantly by the distraction. The rabbit moved closer to her and pressed its small forehead against one of her legs. The Princess watched the animal suspiciously to see what it was doing, confused as to how the rabbit could even see her when she could not even see herself. If only it were not so dark there so she could get at least one answer.

As if the very walls of the castle were listening to her thoughts, small orbs of light shot from her chest and lined the ceiling all the way down the path, creating a soft glowing light to guide her way.

"What in the hells was that?" she whispered, pulse quickening with adrenaline. She felt fur against her leg once more before the rabbit began hopping away. With a lingering look, the rabbit beckoned her to follow.

She chased after her guide until they approached a door that stood slightly ajar, a sliver of light shining through from the other side. The rabbit stopped in its tracks and turned to give the Princess warning. She summoned what little stealth she had, danger loomed on the opposite side of the open door and sent chills along her body. Before she began to move toward it, she noticed the rabbit's ears move as if they were waving to her. She looked directly into the Princess' eyes as she continued twitching her long ears over and over, signaling to her that she must listen.

When the Princess understood, they moved forward side by side. The silence continued even as they moved, odd that not even the gravel cracked beneath her gentle steps. The Princess tried focusing on any sound that could possibly come from the other side of the door, she needed some kind of idea as to where she was headed, if it was even safe.

Then, the tenor of a man's voice caught her attention. Filled with authority but laced with fear, it grew steadily louder in her ears and she pressed on.

"This is treason. You will be executed for your actions today. You have murdered countless civilians below, the very people you evidently want to rule for yourself," a familiar voice raged.

"There will be no executions on my end, I can assure you." A second man responded; his tone coated in a cool confidence. His voice sparked a chilled terror in her veins. This man was evil incarnate—she could sense it immediately.

"You're so sure that you have won today? My wife's family is blessed by the Gods themselves; you fool. The throne will not accept you as long as her blood graces this land." His wife that is blessed by the Gods? How could she not have recognized her father's voice the second he spoke? More importantly, who was the man he was speaking to that clearly intended to usurp the throne?

"Well then, I suppose I should solve that problem, hmm?" A shoe scuffed across the floor as the man turned on his heels, "You! Bring her in." She moved closer to the edge of the door to see inside, moving as silently as a mouse. The room before her was her mother's study. The stained-glass windows reached the ceiling and gave view to the castle gardens. The floor was draped in a snow bear's pelt, dyed a deep red to match the cushioned chairs. She could see her father behind the desk where the Queen did her work, but she was still unable to see the man with which he was speaking to.

Another door across the study sprang open, two guards squeezed in with the disgruntled Queen held between them. Her blonde hair was pulled from her elegant braids and her gown was torn down one side, as if she had been attempting to escape but intercepted. The guards dragged the monarch across the floor until the three of them stood on the red, snow bear skin, gripping the Queen's arms so tightly they were already bruised.

The Princess found it incredibly difficult to slow her rapid breaths, sensing that nothing good was about to come. How could she stand to watch whatever this man planned to do to her mother and not intervene? But she must; with her mother's safety compromised, the Princess must not be captured.

The rabbit gently nudged her legs again, reminding her of her duty to her Kingdom. She felt her tears spill down her cheeks and resisted the urge to wipe her running nose, fearful of making any noise.

She met her mother's glossy blue gaze. The Queen locked eyes with her for only a brief moment, not wanting to bring attention to the Princess. In that shared glance she sent an instruction to her only daughter.

Run, Correa. Keep hidden until you reach the other end of Asvalda. Hone your magic. Prepare for war.

"Your family has ruled quite long enough, I'd wager." He moved closer to the Queen, garnering her full attention as he bent down beside her ear, still only showing the Princess the back of him as he brushed a lock of blonde hair away from her mother's ear, "It is always a mournful day when the reign of a beloved monarch comes to an end. I promise that yours will be nothing short of monumental." With a slow swipe of his hand, he caressed the Queen's throat, leaving behind a path of dark blood pouring down her throat in his wake.

"There is a daughter. Find her and bring her to me." He demanded one of the guards.

The King fell to his knees with a guttural scream that tore from his very soul. Before she was forced to watch the light leave her mother's eyes, the Queen's focus landed on the Princess once more. She received one last message, changing her life forever.

Correa, run.

PART ONE

ONE
BREE

Most mornings, I enjoy sipping my tea in the cozy wicker chair on my porch, looking out at the early morning sun as it shimmers over the sea. This morning, however, I am determined to find my husband and start some trouble. Bringing my tea with me in my favorite cerulean-painted mug, I skip down the front steps of my seaside cottage on a mission to find Destrin—my tall, broody husband who is most likely chopping wood or weapon training.

Weapon training is a staple in our family. Pa owns the most well-known smithy in Western Asvalda, so it's customary that we create our own weapons and learn to use them properly. There aren't many threats on our small island, but Nan taught everyone here the importance of being prepared for an attack or the possibility of being drafted for war. Destrin, having married into the Ragna Clan, took to his weapon training phenomenally well, winning Pa's blessing almost immediately. Of course it helped that he was a soldier in the kingdom's army when we met.

Walking along a small path driven into the dirt by generations of seaside strolls, I spot his muscular frame, chopping wood as expected. I take a few moments to appreciate his broad, muscular stature. He isn't wearing a shirt. Each muscle is honed to perfection, currently shining in the sun from sweat, pronouncing the hard lines even further. I could watch the way his back flexes all day and never grow tired of it, just imagining his bulky arms wrapped around me in a warm, loving embrace.

I huff a longing sigh and twist my long dark braid around my fingers, raptly getting his attention. He wipes the sweat from his forehead above his thick black brows while turning to see me standing on the path, leaning against an old maple tree and taking another sip of tea. His chocolate-brown eyes, made molten by the sun, take me in from top to bottom as slowly as he can muster. Deep lines had set on his forehead, possibly from the strenuous physical labor, or maybe something more. Whatever it may be, I'm sure he'll fill me in at some point, but it seems to be quickly leaving the forefront of his mind as he continues to look me up and down. Seeing the way he looks at me like it is the first time, never ceases to make my heart flutter and my cheeks flush.

Laying down his axe, he grabs a pile of wood larger than my entire torso, and stalks over to my spot beneath the shadow of the leaves. "You look extra delicious, just in case no one has told you yet today, wife." He whispers in a dangerously seductive tone as he walks by, brushing his shoulder against mine.

"I *have* already been told on three separate occasions." I counter with a snarky smile.

"Oh, have you now? And who is it that I need to threaten today?" He sets the freshly chopped wood on the ground and crosses his flexed arms over his broad chest, reaching one hand up to flatten his beard. "Could it be the old fellow by the river this time? Or perhaps our good friend Wallace?" He teases with a knowing smirk.

"It was your very own best friend, actually. While I was returning from the market this morning, Leif caught me and said, 'My, Bree. You look absolutely ravishing today, may I have a bite?'"

"Okay, well, now you've done it." And suddenly, he's chasing me outside the garden. I tip-toe around the edges of the soil, trying not to trip and fall into Pa's flowers. He would have me on flower duty for a month if I crushed any of his favorite Irises. Pa pours his heart and soul into the greenery that surrounds our neighboring cottages, and his hard work shows in the magnificent beauty the flowers bring to the scenery. He's such an excellent gardener that the entire village pays him to create similar works of art in their yards as well. But Irises, those are closest to his heart.

I turn onto the flat stone path that separates the greenery from the beach when the hem of my dress is pulled abruptly, making me trip over my own feet. "Destrin, stop fooling around! I'm going to fa–" I'm interrupted by forceful laughter as Destrin catches me in his strong arms and hurls us both to the ground, tickling me senseless. Well, there goes the rest of my morning tea. At least the mug looks unbroken, laying sideways in a mound of soil.

"I'm sorry, love, I thought you said my best mate noticed how delicious you are? I can't say I blame him, but now I'll have to have some words with both of ya." As he stands, he pulls me up with him, planting a soft kiss against my lips. I love our moments like this; they're so genuine and carefree. Then he will end it with the typical rear grab in about three, two, one, and there it is.

"You'll have your words when we go to the pub after chores tonight, although I suspect he'll have no idea what you're talking about." I say while looking up at him, my arms still wrapped around his neck, and our lips close enough to share a breath, "I haven't seen the man since yesterday."

He raises a brow at my confession—no doubt pondering how he will deal with my trickery. "You will be the death of me, woman." He separates from me and gathers the wood he needs to carry to the cottage, "Where has Annie gotten to today?" He looks down towards the beach as he asks, a usual haunt for our daughter—only five years old–with her shining cinnamon hair and sun-kissed freckled cheeks.

"She's with Pa by the shore, with the other little ones. She saw Samuel with a beautiful shell and is now determined to find her own."

After picking up my discarded mug, we start walking at a slower pace. As we head back to our cottage, I can't help but look up at my husband and think how grateful I am for a man like him. We met when we were barely of age, him being a couple of years older than me. Running through the woods near the fishing village of Skogby, I had fallen and landed directly onto a sharp branch that pierced deep into my calf. He heard my screams from the outskirts of the village and ran toward the noise. Once he discovered me, he carried me back to Pa's smithy, where he helped my grandfather remove the branch and clean the wound.

He offered to row me over the small channel between Skogby and Gledibyr and escort me home. He used this opportunity to tease me endlessly for landing on the only upright stick in the entire forest, and we haven't been rid of each other since. Thank the Gods for that because he has given me the most beautiful family anyone could ask for.

Of course, Annie doesn't look anything like us. Most mothers hope to see themselves in their baby's face, but I didn't get so lucky. I have hazel eyes and waves of dark brown hair, so graciously styled by the salty breeze of our home every day. Destrin has wavy black hair with chocolate eyes, while Annie has my Nan's auburn hair, bright green eyes, and angel-kissed cheeks. I must admit that I am envious of my daughter's freckles, Destrin and I both have smooth, spotless complexions.

I suppose I wouldn't say Destrin has *spotless* skin; he has a short black beard and a jagged scar across his forehead, narrowly missing his eye. He once got into a match of the egos with a drunk who had a blade. The man managed to cut him right down the middle of his forehead, just above his left eye. The village healer was able to close the wound quickly, but not swift enough to help with the new scar blemishing his ruggedly handsome face. The man was left with a bruised eye and wounded ego after Destrin knocked him out cold with one more punch.

We finally reach the woodshed, where my husband stacks the wood with the rest of the pile and turns toward me with a sheepish grin. A look that can only mean one thing, he's about to say something that will leave me less than thrilled. To further prove my theory, he begins fidgeting with his golden arm ring and puts most of his weight on one leg, looking like he suddenly would rather be talking about anything else.

"Out with it," I demand, feigning annoyance. His countenance transforms into a worried grimace as he prepares for whatever news he plans to tell me.

"Pa has mentioned a significant amount of new orders at the smithy. They've mostly come from outside villages—hearing stories of a mysterious woman that scares the piss out of 'em. They want new weapons, *better* weapons, and they want to learn to defend themselves."

Irritation contorts my face–already sensing where this is going. "And why is this a worry for us?"

"Well, we think based on some stories that it might be Tessa, and I just thought it was worth telling you."

Tessa. The woman who brought me into the world and then left me alone in it. She hasn't made an appearance since we received news that Nan had been killed by the Regent during a routine trip to the market in Skogby. Tessa stayed for the ceremony we held for Nan on the shore the following day—as she was a highly respected member of our village—and then my mother fled. That was almost six years ago, Annie was soon to be born and I hadn't even been married to Destrin for a year.

For a long time, we let our heartbreak consume us. We had just lost Nan to the wretched usurper, and then Tessa abandoned us. Pa barely ate for months, and I developed a fondness for ale. These days, Pa hopes to see Tessa again, and I am only fueled by rage when I think of her. I don't think anyone can blame me after what her ex-husband, Bane, put me through.

"Why would I care if my mother is telling ghost stories to villages around Asvalda? Why would I even care to hear that she may even be alive? What a shame that would be."

"Bree, I understand and I'd probably feel the same if I were in yer shoes." Destrin looks at me with a careful gaze, seemingly caught off guard by my bluntness, even when directed at my mother. It is out of character for me, even with my feelings toward her. But when you're abandoned by someone who is supposed to love you more than anything in this world, it can be hard to feel anything but bitter betrayal.

"I think it's justified to have some harsh words when it comes to Tessa. She broke Pa to pieces, and she doesn't know her granddaughter. We went through so much horror together because of Bane. We had just begun mending our bond when she left him, and then she just left? No explanation, no warning, no goodbyes." Tears begin to form, and I try desperately to keep them contained. I have cried enough tears for my mother–*because* of my mother.

Destrin walks over to me and pulls me into a tight hug, kissing the top of my head. He attempts to get a laugh out of me by aggressively sniffing my hair as he always does when he gets the chance; the man is obsessed with the almond soap I use.

"I get it, love, I do. I'm sorry I brought her up. I just figured I'd save the poor soul who might have mentioned her without you being properly warned. The lad wouldn't have stood a chance."

I huff a laugh and shove him away, thankful for his aptitude at casting aside my fury. Taking a few steps forward, I look past the gardens in our shared yard with Pa, and off toward the sea that supplies our village with fish and plenty of stories. I spot Annie and her friends as Pa leans against a large maple tree, watching over them. Annie has a look of pure determination spread across her tiny features as she digs through the sand close to the water's edge, desperate to find a beautiful shell.

I suppose it's worth finding out what else he knows..."Did any of them say what she looks like? Why do you assume it is Tessa?" My tone loses its poison, calmed from Destrin's embrace and watching my daughter explore.

"They said it was a middle-aged woman who spoke ill of the Regent—how he's killing us all. She spoke of magic and creatures that haven't been in these parts for centuries." He pauses and takes a deep breath, coming closer again to take my hand, practically whispering, "She spoke of the true Queen, lost and hurt, needing to be found and brought home."

At this, I go completely still and dare not breathe as I wait for Destrin to continue. In no world would my mother be that reckless. If this is true, she will get us killed by attracting the attention of the usurper.

"That's what makes us think it's her. She sounds like she's gone off the deep end. Pa wants to try and bring her home, ensuring the safety of us all."

My nostrils flare and my cheeks grow hot in response. "And get himself hurt or killed in the process? She doesn't want to be found, Des, we tried. He'd only get his heart broken again when he returns without her, and I'm not sure he'll recover from that again."

"I think you should speak to him, Bree. He's a worried man who wants to find his daughter. Something I know you'd want too." He gives my hand a comforting squeeze, reminding me that he's my anchor, "I'll support whatever you decide. Just keep your mind open, please." He ends the conversation with a quick kiss on the top of my head and whispers, "I love you." As he entwines my fingers with his and starts walking us down toward the beach.

My mind races in a thousand directions, processing everything Destrin has said and what it could mean for us. What will the future hold? If it *is* Tessa, what exactly does she know that warrants such an odd warning of destruction and death to us all? If something is coming, then our village needs to prepare. Pa and Des do what they can, but not enough of the village are properly trained to wield a weapon, let alone fight with one. Tessa is one of the most intelligent people I've ever known. She's not going crazy—she's scared and knows something. So why wouldn't she come back to warn her family? The stories she tells would put a target not only on her back, but on my whole family's as well.

The Ragna Clan guards the most important secret in all of Asvalda. A secret that has the ability to turn the tides of the very structure of our kingdom. Almost half a century ago there was an unwarranted change of leadership.

The Regent has been looking for someone ever since, and we are the only ones who know what happened to her.

TWO
BREE

The sky praises us with her light, and the air carries floral hints throughout the island. A perfect day to bring Annie to the beach by our home and tending to the outdoor chores.

Unfortunately, *I* shall not be allowed either opportunity since my grandfather has made plans for the two of us. He wishes to speak to me about my thoughts on Tessa's ghost stories and what I plan to do about it. I can already hear his attempts to get a feel for the situation—to see what he can get away with doing himself before I stop him.

Pa is getting older, and while he's still incredibly able-bodied and has the stamina of a man twenty years younger, I wish he would start delegating some of his laborious chores. For my sake if nothing else. I'm constantly reminding the man that I need him to stick around for a while longer, that he's the only blood relative in reasonable traveling distance I have left.

My plan was to avoid Pa for a few hours and peacefully pretend that I have no inkling about what may or may not be happening in Skogby. Normally a walk all the way to the end of the beach would do the trick, especially if I wander into the forest it fades into. The island's population of jovial fire sprites reside past the cover of the trees, and they are an absolute joy to be around.

Before I'm able to escape, my traitor husband asked Annie if she wanted to build the Kingdom's castle, Dragon's Peak, in the sand, giving Pa the opportunity to steal me away.

His tanned skin glows brilliantly in the sun, displaying years of working outdoors. His crow's feet and laugh lines are deep enough to give the sea floor a run for its money. The scruff of facial hair that lines his jaw is the same shade of white as his last few hairs that are trying desperately to continue to grow on his balding scalp. He's making sure to walk quicker than normal without taking his eyes off me, knowing my habit of avoidance too well.

"Good morning, Pa. To what do I owe the pleasure this morning?" I ask with a touch of sarcasm and a genuine smile.

"Oh, cut the shit, Bree. I saw the look on your face when Destrin was speakin' with you over here, only Tessa makes you look like that." How dare he know me so well; I need to be more aware of my facial expressions around him, "Thought I'd catch ya before ya go runnin' off to wherever it is you go." He added with a soft smile and side eye.

"Well it was worth a shot feigning ignorance. Best-case scenario it worked. Worst case you make me deal with this immediately instead of tabling it for a day or two." He chuckles at that, the noise a deep gravel.

"What am I gonna do with you?" He has been asking this multiple times a day for the last twenty years at least.

"Well, I'm hoping you'll at least buy me a pint before further souring my mood over our absent loved one. Perhaps two, that may be for the best." I look at him with round, pleading eyes. I feel like a child again when we banter, but it is his doing since he typically gives in to my nonsense.

The Serpent Sound is all that separates Gledibyr from the mainland of Asvalda. It's generally a calm strip of sea, only developing deadly waves in great storms. The water runs mostly clear, casting a turquoise hue to everything beneath and allowing us to see significant depths compared to other parts of the sea.

My husband sits on the other end of the boat, rowing us toward the shore. His onyx hair shines brilliantly under the morning sun, pieces falling from the leather tie he used in an attempt to tame his mane. The rays from the sun make his eyes glow like amber, consuming the largest of my doubts as we sail the familiar route. His aura radiates tranquility and confidence—an aspect of him that has continuously aided my anxiety over the years. A simple smile from him is similar to an embrace, a smile that conquers his face now as he notices my nerves.

"What do you expect to find here, my love? What answers are we looking for?" He asks, looking behind him to gauge the distance.

For a moment a deep sigh is all I can muster while trying to decide the main objective for today.

"I have so many questions for Tessa. I don't know where to begin," I say with uncertainty. "Tessa is telling these tales with purpose, which is my biggest concern. Is it fear causing her to come so close to spilling our secrets? She knows our family will hear these stories and suspect her, so what does she want us to find? Why won't she come home?"

Skogby is fast approaching and we continue rowing in silence, allowing me to dig deeper into my curiosities. A grim thought leaps into the forefront of my mind—what if this isn't Tessa, but a ploy? Once again, that would call into question the coincidence of a lost queen being mentioned so close to the home of those who know her whereabouts. I only allow the thought to traverse my mind for a second longer before refusing to think of it again. My focus must be on finding her, nothing else. If this is a trick then we'll handle it swiftly.

We tie our canoe to the dock, grabbing our packs as we climb out. This particular dock is older with moss lining the edges—the middle of the wooden boards bowing deeply enough to cause concern on whether or not it is structurally sound. I would have preferred Des had chosen one that was built more recently, but today is Harbor Day, so they're all occupied.

Once a week, a larger vessel sails from Skogby to Harbor Isle, the main trading port of the kingdom. It's only accessible by crossing Freya's Fjord, or by land, but you'd have to travel around the Fjord and pass through three other major towns and two forests. Wares from all over the world can be found there, treasures and ales found nowhere else in the kingdom, specifically to encourage tourism. Rumor has it, there's also a slave trade operating in secret, buying and selling thralls to the nobles of the land. This began once the Regent usurped the throne—the late King and Queen would have never allowed such atrocity to blemish their land.

We wander past the rows of fishing docks toward the main market where close to a hundred stalls line the streets. Gledibyr is known for surviving primarily off of our scaly friends, and we take pride in the careful treatment of them before sales. Here in Skogby, while still considered a small village by Asvaldan standards, they have double the number of fishermen for hire, double the amount of fish and only half of the respect we give our coming meal.

My nose is assaulted by the smell of fish, fresh and rotting. Some vendors don't care as much about their product as others, and the evidence is noticeable on this stretch of the aisle. I'll give them the benefit of the doubt, as it is a particularly hot day and the sun is beating down upon us all. Although, other vendors have found ways to keep their product as fresh as possible. Some have stacked chunks of ice beneath their product, while others decorate their boxes with certain flowers to help keep any bugs away, marigolds seem to be a favorite. As we walk by these stalls, the flies incessantly buzz around our heads, and the vendors appear unwashed and miserable as they fail to shoo the bugs away.

Some of my favorite vendors have inhabited these aisles for as long as I can remember. We fish at home, but we don't gather nearly as many delectable creatures compared to the fishermen of Skogby. A huge row of stands showcase giant crabs, lobsters, and even shrimp that have been caught in the Serpent Sound and Freya's Fjord alike. Further down there are tables selling fishing supplies: huge weighted nets, intricate wooden lobster traps, woven baskets, and a significantly better smell.

The stall I'm always most excited to visit is stationed at the end of the market, saving the best for last, in my opinion. The pearls are harvested by the stall owners, a husband and wife duo that are good friends with Pa. They shine beautifully in the sunlight, reflecting the allure of the seas. Pa has gifted the ladies of our family many necklaces and earrings with these pearls over the years. They have a small water table set up behind the stall where kids can learn how to harvest their very own pearls. If the child is successful, they gift them with a small necklace that contains an oval shaped cage to house the pearl. Annie tried for her first time last year but wasn't quite strong enough. I assume she'll ask to try again in the near future. It's too bad we left her behind with Pa for this outing.

Most of the people who live here in Skogby are incredibly friendly, especially to outsiders. This is why it's odd when a particularly grungy fisherman eyes me with a threatening stare as we pass. He has long, matted gray hair with a stringy mess of a beard to match. I may be paranoid, but he looks as if he recognizes me and is far from happy about it. His distaste for me is only heightened when he spits the chew tucked behind his lip onto the ground considerably close to my feet, narrowly missing me and causing me to trip trying to avoid it. He whispers something to his partner lounging beside him, looking just as filthy. Destrin doesn't notice the man, only me tripping and he places his hand on my waist to steady me as we continue on.

We turn down another path leading to the shops and some well known taverns. Pa's Smithy is just down the road; where he works most of the week. "I figure we'll start right from the source. We can ask the shop owners what they've heard and go from there," I say with determination.

Destrin nods in agreement and follows me into the textile shop next to the smithy. I've seen the owner, Glenda, only a few times in the last five years because I cannot make it to the mainland as often since having Annie. Nonetheless, she recognizes me immediately and is just as excited as always to have me visit her. When I was a child and came to town with Pa, Glenda would invite me over to her shop and help her organize fabrics. In return, she would gift me some snacks and coins to go buy us some desserts from the bakery nearby.

"Bree Ragna! It has been much too long since you have visited me. I'm incredibly disappointed! And where is young Annie?" The portly woman pulls me into a tight hug, her ginger hair pulled into a loose bun, barely reaching my chin.

"I left her at the cottage with Pa today. I'm here for some business, Glen." I say as she breaks the hug, looking me over with her bright blue eyes and deepening wrinkles along her brow and beside her eyes.

"Sellin' more maps, are ya? People always ask about them, sayin' they heard the best map maker in all of Asvalda sells custom pieces here on occasion." She teases with a proud smile.

The maps she speaks of are my profession, cartography. Pa told me that when I was a child, I would look at Nan's old maps every day, pretending to go on adventures with my toy animals. As I grew up, I began to learn the details of creating maps and knew I wanted to make them for a living. It's an odd job; cartography is a recent concept in the smaller villages and towns like ours, something that still isn't widely used unless you travel to our capital city, Valderra. Most adventurers still rely on the position of stars and the sun to navigate, which I have found to work quite well overseas, but it's not as useful on land.

With a lack of popularity around these parts, and minimal travel across Asvalda, I wouldn't say I'm the best cartographer in the land. My customers mostly appreciate the designs I provide more than where the nearest lake is located.

"You flatter me, Glen. Today is not about maps but rather some concerning stories plaguing our villages. Have you heard anything strange?"

Her welcoming smile slips into a cautious look, her once fluid movements now shifty and tense. She turns and walks behind the counter, adjusting her display awkwardly.

"You know I pay no mind to the tales these villagers string together, Bree. Listening to those drunk fools only causes stress for a woman like myself." She stops fidgeting and looks into my eyes with a hard, worried stare. I harden my gaze, seeing right through her charade. With a deep sigh, she continues, "I don't know the details, but I have seen people flocking to your Pa's smithy more than usual. Even a few lasses' huddled together have made their way there."

Women going to a smithy for weapons is not unheard of in my village and some of the larger cities in Asvalda. But this is extremely odd for Skogby, where their main focus is their ability to fish and craft.

"Even just that is a help to us, Glenda. Thank you, and I promise to visit more often." I say with a smile as Destrin and I turn to leave.

"And you better bring that, Annie, too! Can't be havin' her forget Ma Glen!" She hollers—any of her previous discomforts vanished.

After hours of talking to various villagers, we're no closer to finding Tessa. We walk into the most famous pub in the main village for dinner, The Angler's Cove. This is where all the men come to drink, gossip, and find a good lay amongst the few widows who drown in the ale every evening. They have the Society of Widowed Women for those who have lost their husbands to the sea while fishing for the giant game, but a few have not been able to cope well, and this is where they choose to loiter. I hold no judgment over them; I acted similarly after Nan had died and Tessa ran. I didn't sleep around, as I was in love with Destrin, but the ale helped keep my sorrow at bay. Or so I thought. Really, it just deepened the grief and gave me horrible headaches.

We sit in a booth against the sidewall of the pub, right in front of a large window with a magnificent view of the Fisherman's docks. This also gives us a clear path to hear any whispers at the bar, where the biggest gossips of them all tend to sit. The young barmaid, I believe her name is Lucille, comes over to take our order of fried salmon with chips and a pint of ale each. The bar is packed, many of the fishermen have anchored for the evening and are here to get properly drunk before heading home to their families. This immediately works in our favor, as two men at the bar start whispering something interesting.

"She's psycho...that woman. Whoever she belongs to needs to get a hold of her before the Guard catches word of her story tellin's."

"Agreed, if my wife ever went off spewing stories about giant serpents and assassins I'd ship her right off to Harbor Isle and hope a

Dread washes over me, forcing me to rush Destrin out of the doorway, eager to be out of the man's gaze, and away from his oppressive stare. As we head back toward Pa's smithy, I decide it is time to bring out some reinforcements.

The secret we keep would have me burned at the stake if found out, and my magic would be a dead giveaway. I can summon a familiar at will and see through his eyes if necessary. The origin of this magic would be a mystery to most since only the Royal Family has abilities, and that is why it is so dangerous. I look down next to my feet and see my sweet loving boy, Mead. He is a large black house cat with pastel green eyes and one white patch of fur on his belly. He weaves between my legs and rubs his soft face against my shin. I bend down to pet him and give him his assignment for the night.

"Mead, we will be staying the night here. I need you to keep exploring the village and look out for any clues of Tessa." I scratch under his chin. He replies with a soft mewl and strolls off into the shadows.

We head into the smithy where I am instantly hit with the smell of pine and leather. Pa keeps the place incredibly tidy, much like his cottage at home and has sprigs of pine hanging all over the place for the fresh fragrance. There is a small apartment upstairs for when he is here too late to sail back home where will be staying.

Once we are upstairs, Destrin sprawls out onto the bed, his ankles crossed and his arms behind his head. He looks at me with tired eyes and smiles gently.

"You are so beautiful, Bree."

"The most beautiful girl you've ever seen?" I tease.

"Of course, nothing can ever compare to your beauty. I could be faced with the sun setting over the Mountains of Frostheim, making the water of the Great Lake glimmer peacefully, and it still could not compare to the raw beauty that is you." I roll my eyes but cannot stop the blush that spreads across my cheeks.

He gets off the bed and slowly walks over to me. Holding my chin between his fingers, he gently lifts my head to look up at him. I take in his strong, chiseled jaw covered by a dusting of black hair. His eyes bore into mine, overflowing with love and adoration.

"The fields of Spring flowers across Asvalda could never smell as sweet as you or look half as beautiful." He kisses the side of my jaw. "Nor could the sands of Einherjor bring such warmth as you." He trails more kisses down my neck, making my eyes flutter shut, and my body melt into his touch. His free hand gently glides down my arm and onto my lower back, moving us toward the bathing room where a large tub and half melted candles reside. The hair on his jaw tickles my ear as he whispers in a raw, gravelly voice, "You are my personal Valkyrie, and I will follow you across the Nine Realms into eternity. For now though, I think I will just follow you into the bath."

THREE
BREE

The dirt from Skogby's narrow alleyways pack tight between the cat's toes, making it challenging to retract his claws as he walks. His gait is slow and careful as he roams the darkened streets of the fishing town, with only the moon lighting his way. Over the last few hours he has not seen or heard anything suspicious that may lead him to his purpose, just trash filled alleys and mice that feast in them. Skogby is sleeping, even the night owls.

His steps are silent and his black fur helps him blend in with the shadows. Almost every nook and cranny has been explored—searching for any clues to give to his summoner. During his retreat from a particularly fresh smelling meal left outside, he spots a new path he has yet to travel. He would have missed the entrance entirely if he hadn't wandered into the street glowing under the moon. This alley is smaller than the others, the walls curve inward and rather than leading to an adjacent street, it leads toward the forest. The cat decides to walk down the alley, as all of the others have proven to be useless in his search.

As he makes his decision, a mouse scurries by, close enough to touch his lowered tail. His green eyes latch onto the creature—fighting between his instinct to hunt and his mission to watch. He allows it to escape, promising that if opportunity arises again, he will indulge. A sharp sound interrupts his thoughts, snatching his attention to the undiscovered path.

Footsteps.

No one is around him, no source of the sound can be located. He has not seen a human in hours—not heard anything but mice in hours. The alley remains empty, yet the steps echo in his mind like they did in the darkness moments ago. The fur along his spine bristles as a freezing chill flows through the alley, bringing with it a sense of foreboding. Against his better nature, he follows the sound. Obscured by shadow once more—paws tense from dirt and stealth—he crouches close to the ground, stalking a prey he cannot see.

The footsteps sound again, now behind him. It's startling enough that he jumps, landing in the direction from which he just came. His eyes focus back on the street, darting from one detail to another in a panic. He has only ever been the predator, whatever is playing games with him is humbling. He doesn't dare move—waiting to see where the footsteps come from next. He expected it might occur behind him once more, whoever this is thrives on his fearful confusion. What he didn't expect was the rustling grass from the opposite end of the alley—moving away from him.

With his ears pinned to his head and underbelly grazing the dampened dirt floor, the cat takes careful steps toward the forest—scanning the space between the town and the trees. The forest is still, no breeze or nightlife disturbs its beckoning silence. Keeping to the backend of buildings, he slinks from shadow to shadow in search of the threat. His eyes never leave the edge of the forest, determined to pinpoint the hiding place of this new arrival.

He doesn't realize how far he searches until he happens upon the familiar scent of his summoner. Allowing a glance above him, it occurs to him that he made it all the way back to the smithy, where his summoner sleeps soundly in the apartment above, with the window slightly cracked. He wonders how he could have stalked an invisible threat this far down without a single hint of whoever he heard. Even more concerning was that he was completely unaware of his surroundings the entire time.

Fear floods his veins. Not for himself—as he cannot be harmed—rather for his other half, Bree. A snapping branch sends his small heart into a flutter and brings his attention back to the forest. He frantically searches for something—anything. The moment he thinks to return home and give warning, he spots a small flicker between the trees. Surely he should gather more information before inviting her to this danger, and so he strides toward the ominous flame to do the best that he can.

Approaching the fire he notices two distinct details. One, the air is so thick and dense that he feels as if he is being pushed into the ground. Two, no warmth radiates from the flame—for it is not even real.

The fire disappears and with it, any chance of escape. But the cat is held by an invisible force, unable to even turn his head or stretch his toes. All he can hear is the rushing of his blood as it roars in his ears and the quick pattering of his heart that tries to jump from his chest. A whimper escapes the poor creature's throat as whatever holds him in place tightens.

A poisonous chuckle breaks through his tremors, even his blood seems to have dammed its course through him. Another phantom flame circles around his trapped body, closing in on him and fueling his fear. It's then the cat spots the source of this craze—a face glowing in the flame. Matted hair frames his hollowed cheeks and a stringy beard speaks to his lack of bathing. He towers over the cat, but lessens the distance as he bends at the knees. He pulls a small knife from his pocket, his thumb running along the twine wrapped handle almost lovingly.

The knife is held against the cat's throat, promising a sick, disturbing violence. Before he can injure the creature, his lips spread across his face in a menacing smile. His rotting teeth are exposed in the firelight, fresh blood from his cracked lips leaking into his mouth-—face now only an inch from his. With a voice as cracked as his lips and deep with power, he whispers into the night.

"*Hello,* Princess.*"*

My eyes shoot open and I sit up, drenched in a cold sweat with my heart racing a million beats per minute.

"Mead, come home." I gasp, my voice so shaky I can hardly recognize it as my own. The black cat appears at the end of the bed—shaking uncontrollably. His fur stands on end as I stroke his back, willing my breath to match my slower movements.

"Destrin, wake up." I shove him over so he's on his side and he groans in exhaustion, peeling his eyes open to look at me.

"What's happened? Are you alright?" I must look awful, fear completely taking over my aura because he immediately sits up, and his attention darts to Mead. "Did Tessa do something to him?"

"Not Tessa. A man from the market today. He spit at me as we walked past. I brushed it off thinking he was just a grumpy old man who doesn't like outsiders. Then he was at the pub. I didn't see him there until we were leaving, when I felt him staring at me again, with pure rage in his eyes. Mead was out walking around the village, and this same man stalked him and trapped him in the forest with magic."

My lungs tighten, making my breaths quick and shallow. My muscles tighten as well, tension radiating from my neck to my shoulders, making me almost numb. I run to the bathing room the second my skin becomes clammy and my mouth fills with saliva, and I throw up in the bathtub. Destrin follows closely behind, holding my hair out of the way just in time.

"Shhh, Bree, it's okay, I'm here. We are safe inside, just keep Mead in for the rest of the night." He tries soothing me by rubbing my bare back with his firm hands. When I finally gather the will to speak, my lip trembles with my words.

"He was watching our bedroom window. And…"

I don't want to repeat what the man said out of fear that if *I* speak it out loud, my entire world changes. *Annie's* entire world changes. We knew of the danger, and that danger has found us, "He…he called me Princess." A wave of unexpected, eerie calm washes over me after admitting the words. All emotions drain from me as I look into my husband's eyes and try to accept the turn my life is about to take. My resignation is not closely matched by Destrin , whose eyes widen and stretch in denial.

"What do you mean? How can he…that is impossible Bree." He begins pacing back and forth between the bathroom and bedroom, his hand scratching against his jaw and his mind moving at an impressive speed.

"I swear it, Destrin. He looked thrilled when he trapped Mead, like he won a bet." He shouldn't have even suspected what Mead is, let alone that I was seeing through him. He looks and acts like an ordinary house cat, the only difference being that he cannot die.

"We need to get home unseen. We'll plan our next move in order to protect you and Annie. Pa will have an idea—he always does."

After I freshen up, we pack our belongings and decide to wait until the sun rises, dawn is only an hour from now. We wait downstairs in Pa's arsenal of weapons until the first birds sing their morning songs. As the first light begins to shine over the top of the forest, Destrin looks to me and gently grabs the back of my neck, pulling me against him.

"No matter what happens Bree, I'll always protect my girls. You two are the most important part of my life, and while I breathe there is nothing that will harm you. I promise you, my love."

I meet his beautiful brown eyes, tears filling mine, and he pulls my lips to his for the most meaningful kiss of my life. I have no idea how I've been so lucky. How I found this man who loves me so wholly that I feel like a goddess under his gaze. If I know anything, it's that this man will be the death of me.

And I him.

We dock the boat on our island after a panicked trip home, *mostly* confident that we weren't followed. Of course, anyone who looked out at sea could spot a small canoe sailing toward Gledibyr, but we can only hope for the best. We agree that we need to be extra cautious, Annie is not to leave our sights for the foreseeable future. We also agree that we need some extra hugs from our little one. Being away from her is hard for us both, and we weren't expecting how much that need would grow as we witness the state of our village when we reach the market.

All of the shop shutters are closed. Black sheets hang from windows and front doors of every home. The streets are void of life—not even the stray cats can be seen creeping in the shadows. The feeling of absolute dread permeates the air so strongly, it makes my blood run cold and limbs heavy. Destrin and I hold each other's hands cautiously. The realization of what is happening washes over us in the same moment.

The village is in mourning.

Something devastating has happened in our absence.

Our hands break apart as we race toward our family cabins, hoping our loved ones have been spared from whatever tragedy took place here. I can't help but think of the last time I saw Annie—how distraught she was that we were going to Skogby without her because she felt something would go wrong.

Ever since she could speak, she's been able to tell us when something was about to happen. She can never pinpoint exactly what it is, but she experiences an onslaught of emotion she'll feel in the future very suddenly. It's a gift that is unheard of by humans, except those blessed by the Gods. Her secret is kept as tightly as mine. Although, it seems our secrets threaten us and we must tread carefully in the coming days.

But what if Annie has already been killed?

That man knew me somehow. Could he also know my family? My baby?

She told us something horrible was going to happen, and while we always heed her warnings, we had expected the ominous event to occur in Skogby while we were there, not so close to home. When Nan was killed, the whole village mourned her for weeks, every building was draped in the same black sheets of death as tonight. Who could have been taken to make them react this way again?

Not my Annie, it couldn't be.

Not the most stable person in my life, Pa.

I can't lose anyone else.

I refuse to.

When we make it to the cottage, Destrin barely gets the door open before we stumble inside and run to Pa's room. Its completely dark; no candles are lit, and our panic heightens while our bodies are still in action. I turn to my left and feel for the dresser I know is there, opening the top drawer where he keeps silly things like old keys, broken quills, and an acorn that looks like an arse. Luckily, he stashes matches here as well.

I light the candles on the ledge of the dresser and turn to the bed. But it's empty. "Pa? Annie? Hels, let the Norns be kind; let them be unharmed." I pray breathlessly.

There is no answer–divine or otherwise. Destrin throws open every door of the cottage, howling Annie's name, searching for our little one in the darkness. I recognize the sobs that sit in his chest, threatening to tear from him. His voice breaks every other call for her. My husband is a stern man who was taught to hide his emotions. Lay a threat to his kin though, and his reaction will be nothing short of deadly.

I almost scream in frustration until the most beautiful sound that has ever graced my ears fills the hall. A voice that shreds all of my fear into nothing, and fills my heart with the warmth that was seeped from it by dread.

"Mommy? Daddy?" the small voice asks.

Destrin and I practically throw ourselves down the stairs to embrace her. I wrap my arms around her tiny body and cry into her shoulder; the relief I feel overwhelming me completely. Destrin holds us both in his massive arms, as close to his heart as he can bring us. We sit there holding each other for what feels like an eternity before I look up into the doorway and see Pa standing there, looking more sorrowful than I have seen him in five years. I separate from Destrin's grasp to hug Pa, finally able to breathe knowing they're both okay.

"What happened? Why is the town in mourning?" I ask him.

The corners of his mouth turn into a deep frown, and his gaze lowers to the floor, holding back quiet tears of his own. Before he can explain, Annie pulls away from her father enough to look at me and explains herself.

"My friends are gone." She says in a small, sad voice.

"What do you mean they're gone, honey?" Destrin asks her, his hand smoothing out the back of her hair.

"The sea took them away from me when we were playing."

My eyes, round in horror, and I look at Pa for confirmation. He brings his gaze back to mine, tears glistening down his sun-tanned wrinkled cheeks. He gives me one sullen nod and runs his fingers through his almost white mustache.

"I tried to save Samuel, Mommy." Her voice breaks as her sadness overtakes her, barely able to keep her voice discernible. "He yelled for me, and he choked on a lot of water. I went to go take his hand, but Pa stopped me, and now they're all gone!"

Des brings her head back to his chest and squeezes her a little tighter.

"I'm so sorry, sweet girl. I'm so, so sorry." They rock back and forth, Annie crying into her father as he rubs her back in wide circles, looking up at Pa.

"Who?" He asks in a deep whisper.

"The Orinson twins, Samuel Sigurdsson, and Bjorn Olafsson." He rasps quietly.

No wonder the entire village is in mourning; we lost some of the brightest, most inspiring children here. They were all under ten years old and promising young boys. The Orinson twins were known for pulling pranks on the locals, but they always came back to help whoever they chose as their victim, making sure they knew they were just teasing. They were good, funny boys, and they dreamed of joining the Asvaldan army in the city of Einherjor.

Bjorn loved to fish with his old man, another sweet boy who treated everyone respectfully, especially Annie, who looked up to him. But Samuel Sigurdsson, this is who broke my Annie's heart the most. They have been best friends since birth, always finding each other as soon as we let them outside to play. They created their own language only they could understand. They pick each other flowers and find each other sea shells on beach days. I believe that if Samuel hadn't been taken from her, they would've never grown apart. He was her rock, and she was his sunshine.

He lost his mother when he was just three years old, so his grandfather, Wallis, took over as his guardian. The two struggled with the void where Samuel's mother should have been, where my closest friend once was. Annie, only two years old, started giving Samuel bear hugs every time she saw him and refused to let go until he smiled. She helped heal his broken heart, and now she needed him to help heal hers.

The Norns have quite a time meddling in our lives, deciding the heartbreak we'll go through and the challenges we'll pass in order to earn our spot in the Godly Realms. I can't help but wonder why they decided to teach my daughter how to experience the death of someone so close to her at such a young age, and what they're preparing her for.

Once everyone is settled, Destrin and I bring Annie into her room to get some rest. She wraps her small arms around her father's neck and rests her head on his shoulder, staring off at nothing in particular with a single tear forming in the corner of her hazel eyes. Today Annie has proven what a strong girl she already is, encountering death face to face and not being afraid, only mournful for the loss of her dear friend.

Destrin lays her onto her small bed and tucks her under the quilt that Nan made many years ago. Although she never got to meet Annie, she knew that someday Destrin and I would have an adventurous and beautiful family. She said she could tell by the way we looked at each other like this was it, our epic love story was just beginning, and nothing would ever get in our way. Nan made this quilt for our children with the intent of telling them our family history. The quilt is beautiful; each square depicting another part of our story. They are designed to look like stained glass, with vibrant colors and soft transitions. We've told her a watered-down story of an adventure with dragons, giant serpents, and princesses. We expressed that it's simply a fairy tale, like the ones other children hear from their parents as well.

The real story tells of a Princess in danger, running to find solace in the shadows. Her parents, the King and Queen, were murdered in a coup with the intent of stealing the crown. The Princess, now technically Queen, found her way to a small village where she met a handsome man. They fell in love, got married, had children, and then grandchildren. So there lived a Queen and two princesses on an island with nothing but the sea surrounding them and the love of their family.

On one square, there's a woman watching her young daughter play with a tiny black cat. This cat was not my familiar, Mead, but a real cat whom I loved very much. Rosie lived a long life with our family, and she was my first and only pet I've ever had. I smile at the memories of her and how my mother's bedtime stories consisted of "Queen Tessa, Princess Bree, and Princess Rosie."

"We're so sorry for what you went through today, my little love." Destrin says as he gingerly brushes her hair behind her ears. "But you are a remarkable young girl, and I happen to know that you can get through anything the Gods throw your way. You are a Ragna, after all, and Ragna women are just built better." At that, he pinches her nose and gives her a slobbery wet kiss on her forehead, coercing a giggle from her. I sit myself down on the end of her bed, placing a hand on her leg over the covers.

"My dear Annie, do you have any questions? Any fears that you can let us carry for you?" I ask.

She shakes her head no and whispers, "I think I just want to say goodbye to my friends. I'm going to miss them so much." Another tear falls silently down her cheek, causing Destrin and me to glance at one another and exchange a nod of understanding. I slide onto one side of her bed, closest to the wall, and Destrin climbs onto the other side, creating a little Annie sandwich.

"We can make that happen Annie. We will go out to the beach so you can say your peace for your friends. We'll bring them offerings and beg the Gods for mercy and an entrance to the heavens."

She snuggles into my arms, facing me, her head in the crook of my arm. Destrin reaches his arms around the both of us, and we lay there until she falls asleep. When it's safe to leave, we sneak out and head to our bedroom to process everything that has happened the last few days and prepare for whatever may come tomorrow.

FOUR
BREE

When I wake up, the birds are singing and the sun casts rays of light through the burlap curtains. I decide to let Destrin and Annie sleep in and tackle the day myself, starting with explaining everything that happened in Skogby to Pa. Between the funeral the town held for the boys and making sure we're taking care of Annie as best as we can while she grieves, I haven't had a chance to speak with Pa about the fisherman and what he did to Mead.

I make a cup of tea in my favorite mug and head over to Pa's cottage next door, knowing he's already awake. He likes to rise before the sun to get an early start on his garden before heading to the smithy for a long day of work.

He's sitting in a rocking chair outside his front door and smiles at me as I walk over to him, taking a seat in the adjacent chair. I admire the large maple tree in our yard and watch a red squirrel scurry up and down the tree as though it's whispering secrets to the birds. I have no idea how to start telling Pa everything that's on my mind, but being the father figure every girl needs, he knows when I am stuck in my thoughts. He could gather two things for sure. One, we didn't come home with my mother like he hoped we would. Two, we came home positively spooked.

"Don't think too hard, Bree. You might break something in that head of yours." I crack a smile as he sips his tea–mischief in his eyes. "What happened in Skogby that has you so hidden in your thoughts?"

"Well, we didn't find a single trace of Tessa beside the stories we have already heard. The barmaid described her, and the woman apparently looks just like her...we stayed the night in your apartment, and I sent Mead out to look for her while we slept." Thinking about the man trapping Mead with me in his mind sends shivers down my spine, and I have to take a deep breath to collect myself.

"There was a man in the market who watched me. Well, he didn't just watch. He glared. He had hate in his eyes, but I've never seen him before, let alone done anything to warrant such malice. I saw him again at The Angler's Cove, and he acted the same. When I was sleeping, I was watching through Mead's eyes." At the mention of him again, I summon the cat for comfort. He curls up in my lap, and I begin to slowly pet his head to ground myself and remember that we're okay–for now.

"He was nothing but a toy in the man's twisted game. He tried confusing Mead until finally, he lured him into the woods. He trapped him—threatened him. Then he looked into his eyes and called me Princess. He was speaking directly to me. I don't understand how he knew Mead wasn't a normal cat, let alone that I was in his mind at that exact moment."

Pa's chair no longer rocks back and forth, and his brow furrows, deepening the wrinkles across his forehead. Pa has always been able to come up with some kind of solution to the most mundane problems; the fact that this one may have him stumped is more than discomforting.

"I'm not sure how he would know, Bree. Your Nan did everythin' she could to keep herself hidden from the Regent. No one shoulda known who she was, or her grandkid. I'm wonderin' if somehow her protection got too weak when she was killed." He leaned forward and rested his elbows on his knees, mug in one hand and his chin in the other.

Nan did have every protection in place for being a Queen on the run. Her real name was Correa Asvalda, and when she was eighteen years old, she had been forced to flee the court when there was a coup against her parents–the King and Queen of Asvalda. In order to ensure that our bloodline remained safe, she fled. If she hadn't escaped, the Regent would have killed her beside her parents–effectively taking the throne *and* absorbing our Blessing from the Gods in one fell swoop. The Queen had told her to prepare for war. Instead, she met Pa. Nan changed her name to Cyn Ragna, and settled down right here in Gledibyr, foregoing her goal of retaking her throne from her parent's murderer. They eventually had my mother, Tessa, and her brother, Jaris, and in order to protect their growing family, she needed to delve deep into the magic she possessed and studied up until she left the castle.

We have no clue whether or not her charms have held since she was killed, and because our magic usually doesn't manifest until the age in which she fled, we were unable to find any information. If this is the case, then I may have led the Regent's men right to our home. He will never stop hunting the Asvaldan heirs, for that is the only way he can truly be the ruler of our land.

When the Gods blessed our family, they placed a unique magic upon us–making the crown only truly ours by blood. The only way someone else can be crowned the true ruler is if they have eradicated the females in the bloodline themselves, leaving no more heirs to rule. Our magic would be transferred to him, but ultimately be cursed by the Gods for defying their chosen. The Regent had somehow finally found Nan, but he hadn't known she had multiple female heirs at that point. He would have only known she had at least one heir when he killed her and the power still didn't transfer to him. We heard many stories of his murderous rampages in the capital, Valderra, when he learned he had no idea how many women he needed to kill to become King. The only way that fisherman could have even known that I'm a princess is if...

"Pa...I think the Regent has my mother, and it's possible she told him about us."

After a few moments of silence, his hands gradually begin to shake so savagely that he drops his mug, shattering on the ground. His face becomes painted in horror as he imagines what terror his only daughter might be facing if she had to give up her family secret and if she really is in the hands of the most dangerous man Asvalda has ever seen.

FIVE
BREE

The village is humming with excitement as everyone begins decorating for tomorrow's Solstice Festival. Women scurry back and forth with ribbons falling from their arms, and men surround fire pits to cook large quantities of meat. Many of the children have been tasked with chores for preparation as well, helping their parents with smaller tasks they haven't gotten to yet. Regardless of all the work needing to be done, everyone has a smile on their face.

The Solstice Festival has always been a fun and lively event in Gledibyr, but this year even more so because it's also a celebration of life for the boys we lost to the sea.

I watch Pa work in villagers' gardens, gathering flowers from each yard to create beautiful bouquets for the tables that will be set up in the middle of the market square. He's as friendly as always with our neighbors, but I can spot the solemn shadow in his eyes as he works quietly. He has been more closed off and determined for answers ever since I told him my suspicions about Tessa and the Regent.

If I'm correct, and I really hope I'm not, there's a possibility that for the last five years, she may have been in the clutches of the most vile man Asvalda has known. And I've been here, angry with her for abandoning us. It would be a cruel fate to escape the clutches of an abusive husband just to be trapped by another monster entirely. If there was the choice, what position would I rather her be in? Battered and bruised by my stepfather, or tortured by a force from Hel. Neither, preferably, but it seems the Norns have weaved a complicated and devastating fate once again.

I try not to let myself dwell on this theory. I don't know if it holds any truth, and it's best not to get myself upset over something I have no tangible proof of. We *will* find my mother and help her if we must, but we need to find answers while keeping the last remaining heirs as safe as possible.

In the meantime, I'll spend this time with my family and prepare for the next steps. I'll savor these next few days of feasting, drinking, and laughing to honor our seasons and the Gods. I walk through the bustling crowd of villagers to find Destrin, moving tables with Annie at his ankles, pretending she's doing the heavy lifting. I sneak up behind her and lightly tug the two braids that Des weaved into her auburn hair this morning. She jumps and turns to face her "attacker" with a silly grin and furrowed brows in an attempt to be intimidating.

"Excuse me, Mommy. I'm busy with Daddy moving tables for feasts!" She chimes in her small but stern voice as she crosses her arms.

"Oh, I do apologize, young Annie. How could I have ever been so rude to interrupt such an important task? Do you mind if I steal your Father for a moment? You seem to be doing most of the work anyway."

She pretends to think carefully over my request, "Yes, I suppose that's alright. But can I go find some kids to play with? I've been helping Dad all day!" She jumps up and down in anticipation. She has been trying to play with other kids in the village she hasn't been as close with since the passing of her dearest friends.

"Of course, you can head home for dinner when the sky turns pink and the sun decides to sleep." I give her a soft kiss on her forehead and send her off.

"Well, now you've got me to yourself. What will ya do with the time?" Destrin asks playfully, stalking over and pulling me into his warm embrace. He's always smelled like pine, just like Pa, and it's one of my favorite, comforting scents in the world. To me it represents comfort and love–safety, even.

"I just wanted a kiss from my little one and a hug from my husband. Is that too much to ask for?" I mumble into his sweaty tunic. He chuckles, and it reverberates through his chest and onto my cheek.

"Wife, if that was all that you wanted, you wouldn't have relieved Annie of festival chores. How can I help you, love?" His hands start gliding through my hair, massaging my scalp.

I turn so my ear now rests on his chest instead, and say with a sly smile, "I suppose a kiss from you would do, as well."

Earning another snicker, he removes his hands from my hair, places one under my chin, and lifts my lips to meet his in a disgusting, wet kiss that he aggressively licks his lips for, "Des! You're insufferable!" I shout with a laugh and attempt to push him away, but the other hand grips my waist and tightens, holding me in place against his body as he laughs with me.

He lowers his face to mine again and gives me a real kiss, entwining his fingers back in my hair with one hand and holding my lower back with the other. It's a kiss that would make any woman think indecent thoughts, so loving and tender but also whispering promises of the night to come.

"I love you, Bree. Now let me finish my chores. It will take me all night now that I've lost my little helper!" He exclaims dramatically.

I playfully slap his bicep and roll my eyes.

"I'll be getting started on dinner. Don't be late, husband!"

Most families eat light dinners the night before seasonal festivals since there will be an abundance of feasting and drinking the following day. Tonight we have Pa over, and eat a simple dinner of roast chicken with some veggies grown from the garden. He doesn't speak much, still too lost in thought. Though, he wouldn't dare speak of any of this in front of Annie anyway.

As we begin to clean the table, Pa catches my attention and gestures to follow him with a quick tilt of his head. I task Annie with helping Des finish the dishes and follow Pa out the front door and onto the path that connects our cottages for some privacy. I stand close enough beside him that I can feel the warmth radiating from him in the evening chill, watching the sea sparkle under the light of the moon, hanging low in the sky tonight. When he doesn't break the silence after a few moments, I look over and witness his silent tears treading down his cheeks. I can count on one hand how many times I have seen my grandfather cry.

"So many things could be wrong, dear. *Everythin'* could be wrong. I can't help but think what Cyn would be doin' if she thought her daughter could possibly be tortured for information. She'd be doin' somethin', not just sitting here preparin' for a festival. What kind of father does that make me if I haven't even been out to help find her?" His voice breaks, sobs wracking his shoulders as they shake with the flowing tears.

I rub my hand in comforting circles on his back, hoping to help calm his breathing. When he regains his composure, he adds, "We need to do somethin', Bree. She's not just my daughter. She's the next Lost Queen after Nan, and we have to find her." His words hit me like a brick to the chest. I can't bear to look at him like this, knowing that I have done close to nothing in pursuit of her–that I have contributed to his desperation to find her. My chin quivers with my realization and I make a vow to make this right.

For me.

For him.

For her.

"I know, Pa, I do. But we also need to keep Annie safe. If the Regent has someone on his side that knows who I am, then they know about Tessa. Maybe they have no inkling of Annie yet, and if it's to stay that way, we need to protect her at all costs." I straighten my posture and raise my chin before grasping his shoulders. "I promise that we'll begin searching for her. But I need you to remember that we have to do this very carefully. No matter what I have felt over the last few years, I love my mother dearly, and I want to help her. But not at the cost of my daughter's safety. Nothing will come before that—for the sake of not only my heart but the future of this country as well. If Nan has taught this family anything, Tessa would agree."

He nods his head in agreement, gives me a tight hug goodnight, and I walk back to my cottage alone. Destrin is already upstairs with Annie, preparing to tell her a bedtime story. When I reach them, I stand in the doorway and watch the two people I love most in the world lay side by side on the tiny child-sized bed, not meant for a six-foot-tall burly man by any means. His right arm rests beneath her head while his left holds the golden armband that the Jarl gifted him as a young boy.

Every child who reaches the age of ten and wishes to be trained as a warrior goes to see the Jarl that rules over them, and he entrusts them with a golden armband that signifies the child's coming journey as a warrior. This tradition is held all across Asvalda, and it's mandatory in order to be permitted to enter the military city of Einherjor.

My eyes float over the two of them as he tells her all of this, and adds the story of his training. "When I was given this armband, I was so excited to go and learn how to properly use a sword. I said goodbye to my family, and was shipped off to Einherjor, where I learned the ways of the warrior."

She takes the band from him and inspects the details of the golden Ouroboros; its mouth is separated from the end of its tail in order to open and fit on one's wrist. "Daddy, did you ever have to fight in a battle?"

He watches her run her finger over the tiny scales of the snake's body, "I did. I fought in one against creatures from another kingdom. It was a very sad period for Asvalda, our army took a devastating hit. It's how I was injured and put on a simple scouting mission near the forest that surrounds Skogby. One day as I was on my way to the market, I found a very clumsy girl in the woods who needed some help of her own."

Annie never heard this story before and she looks at him with wide eyes and a giggle. "What was wrong with her?"

"Oh, turns out she lost her own battle with an upright stick in the ground. I carried her home to her mother and grandfather. I liked her so much that I decided I was going to keep her, and then we made a little gremlin to keep us even more company!" He began tickling her sides, making her gasp for air in hysterics.

In between bouts of laughter she managed to yell in disbelief. "The girl in the woods was Mommy?!"

I decide it's time to make my presence known and walk into the bedroom, sitting on the end of her bed by Destrin's feet. "Yes, it was me, and I lost no battle that day. The stick broke, which I believe means I won."

"The stick may have been broken, my love, but so was your skin, so I think we can at least call it a draw." He counters with a laugh and a twirl of Annie's curly hair. "Anyway, before we got sidetracked,

I was telling you about this armband." He nudges Annie, and she immediately focuses back on the forgotten, golden snake in her hands. "I want you to have this band, Annie. You have been a warrior in your own right the last week, and we're so proud of you. You're a responsible, caring, selfless girl, and we are beyond blessed to be your parents."

He pulls her in for a tight hug, and she attempts to put the band on her upper arm, before it slides back down around her wrist. "I love you, Mom and Dad." She murmurs, and we hold each other close as she falls asleep, golden armband in hand and a content smile on her face.

Destrin

The day my heart refuses to flutter erratically at the sight of my wife will be the day it ceases to beat altogether. She's walking around our bedroom in nothing but a nightgown and I simply want to devour her. Her dark hair trails down her back like silk, and spills over her bare shoulder, covering the thin strap to the garment. She hasn't slept well in the last few weeks, the evidence bruised under her eyes, but her face is still that of an angel. The Gods granted me the highest honor when they put her in my path, weaving our fates together. I couldn't have asked for a better partner or mother of my child. Annie will no doubt be just as strong as her, and the women that came before her.

Bree pulls the thick blankets halfway down the bed, preparing to curl under them and try for another night of fitful slumber. Seeing her stuck in her head for days on end, unsure of what to do next, beating herself up over things she cannot control, haunts me to no end. Instead of undressing and joining her, I fill the bath in the adjoining room and light the candles surrounding the large tub. She pulls her hand away slowly when I come back to her, trying to quietly signal for her to follow me. She forces her exhausted eyes open and reluctantly follows, leaning heavily against me as I guide her into the bathing room. As soon as she feels the heat from the tub, she slips from her nightgown and turns to undress me as well. Unintended on my end, but not unwelcome.

She guides me into the tub behind her, water flowing over the edges since I didn't anticipate us both getting in. I rest my back against the edge, and she places herself between my legs, resting her back and head against my chest. Her limbs go limp as she allows the warmth of the water to relax the tension in her body, and I reach over to grab her soaps to do my part in releasing her tension as well.

I can't get enough of the almond soap she uses for her hair. I pour some water over her and work the almond masterpiece through her thick hair, massaging her scalp in slow strokes. She doesn't stop the moan that escapes her lips, but I'm not a man to complain about something so beautiful. She lets me move her forward to rinse the soap out, and I move some soap over her neck, shoulders, and so on, until she melts under my hands.

I press a kiss to the top of her head and keep her pressed against me. I want her to soak up every drop of love she can, to know that she's not alone, and never will be. I have no idea what will come next for my girls, but I will make sure they have everything they need to succeed.

I can feel the moment she drifts to sleep, her breathing slows and her mouth hangs slightly open. After waiting a few minutes, I carry her off to bed. Once she's tucked beneath the covers I follow close behind into a dreamless sleep, because the woman who has made every dream of mine come true is already snuggled tightly against me.

Bree

There couldn't be a more beautiful day for the Solstice Festival. The sky matches the blue of Pa's hydrangeas, the sun is shining, and there's a soft breeze. I can already hear music playing from the market square as I usher Annie and Des out of the cottage. It's a short walk, but normally we can't hear the everyday hustle from here, which means the celebrations are already heavily underway.

Nearing the end of the dirt path, I see the market has been made to be completely unrecognizable. Large wooden tables fill the wide streets and extravagant bundles of flowers with ribbon graces each one. Gold and seafoam colored ribbons connect to each of the stone buildings from their roofs across from one another, creating a lattice pattern underneath. There are strings with empty glass bulbs woven in between the ribbons; these bulbs will contain the local fire sprites when the night approaches. Usually they agree to help us light our celebrations like this and we pay them with as much food from the feast as they want and a considerable amount of ale. Who wouldn't want a free space where you can eat and drink to your heart's content?

In the middle of the market square is a large sequestered area where the villagers will soon start dancing. The band, consisting of a lyre, a flute and some hand drums, plays just beside this area, and a few of the children are already dancing in circles around them. Annie lets go of my hand to race toward them, and Des quickly takes her place, throwing his arm over my shoulders and pressing a kiss on my temple.

We approach a podium set up in front of the tables where Jarl Borgsik stands, preparing to give the usual speech that signifies the official beginning of the festival. He's a stocky man with brown hair braided close to his scalp on each side, the rest not in the braid reaches his elbows. His beard has small beads made of bones with runes carved into them, and he sports a crooked nose that has been broken many times in battle.

"Everyone gather here, please! Come on, come on, we want to start drinking, don't we?" He hollers to the crowd, earning a cheer in response. We gather around the Jarl, and the entire village grants him their full attention with eager smiles.

"We are starting things off differently this year and will be combining two traditions." Soft whispers rush through the crowd in questionable excitement. "I have some Ouroboros bands I give to the young men who are preparing to ship off to Einherjor–becoming fierce and honorable warriors for our land. It's my understanding there were two young men from this village that planned on making their journey to my homestead this year in order to begin this transition." He pauses and reaches into the pocket of his fur lined cloak to pull out two golden Ouroboros bands, identical to the one Destrin gave Annie last night.

"Will the Orinson family come stand before me, please."

Everyone goes silent, there isn't a single whisper in the air, just emotional tension as we all begin to piece together what two traditions the Jarl is combining. The twins' parents reach the podium beside Jarl Borgsik and he turns to face them. He holds up the bands for everyone to see, and places one in the hands of the boys' father and one in the mother's. "Today, I honor Rolf and Gunnar Orinson by gifting their blood with the Ouroboros bands, signifying them as warriors of the realm. May they feast with the Gods and be remembered with joy. Now, Elsie, please roll the cart so everyone can grab a pint." A thin woman with blonde hair and a generous smile begins pushing a wheelbarrow filled with pints around, offering them to villagers as she passes.

Once everyone has a pint in hand the Jarl continues his speech. "We'll also recognize their friends who were lost to the sea." He raises his pint above his head and looks over the crowd. "To the young boys, Rolf, Gunnar, Bjorn, and Samuel. May the Gods look over you, and you over your families. Skål!"

At that moment, the entire crowd shouts, "Skål," in return. The combined chant sends chills over me. A single cloud covers the sun at the same moment a breeze rustles the trees, and the birds stop their song. Our home is saying goodbye, mourning the loss alongside us. I sip my ale in honor of the boys, and relish in the bittersweet moment of our community coming together for each other, including the land itself.

"They will leave this realm with our celebrations of their lives! Now, may the feasts begin!"

The crowd scatters, and the regular chatter of people begins immediately. Destrin and I find Annie to grab her a plate of food. The whole village sits themselves at the tables set up down the road and we eat, talk, and drink until the sun finally sets. The fire sprites make their appearance, dancing along in the air in a line toward the empty glass bulbs hanging above us. As they fill the bulbs, the square glows a brilliant amber. The crowd cheers and a very homely woman climbs up onto her table with a drink in her hand and a sloppy smile plastered across her face. "Let's dance!" She yells. And at that, the band picks up the pace and everyone makes their way to dance the night into oblivion.

SIX
BREE

The lights spin above me as Destrin twirls me around into his arms, finishing our dance with vigor. We're both covered in sweat and can hardly breathe, but we smile at one another and kiss like we aren't in the middle of the square surrounded by the entire village. Not that anyone would take any notice. Most of our company is piss drunk and kissing strangers while dancing. Many of the men adorned their best ceremonial sword for the occasion in the presence of the Jarl, which are now lying across tables or leaning against buildings as they flail around with their friends and lovers. Some of the women who wore corsets lost them to galivant more comfortably, and many of the children have long since gone to bed.

Someone screams down the road, the ale hitting the swaying dancers, and they are beginning to fall to the ground dramatically.

As late as it is, the celebration, drinking, and dancing continue under the stars. We break apart our kiss, and I look into my husband's chocolate colored eyes. I will never understand how I got to be so lucky as to have a man like Destrin Svanhild. It's a safe comfort, knowing that my daughter has such an honorable man as a father–knowing that he will do anything to protect us, no matter the cost.

Annie finds us, one of the few of her age still awake, and we take a seat at a nearby table. A small group of older women sit beside us, offering warm smiles as they welcome us. Eydis, who supplied most of the ale for the evening, is among the women, sitting closest to us.

Destrin lifts Annie up high into the air and then sets her playfully on his knee, handing her a muffin from a bowl on the table.

"How are ya feelin', little one? Ready to go to bed soon?" he asks.

She shakes her head so forcefully that she dizzies herself, and shoves half of the muffin into her mouth.

"What if I told ya we can sword practice tomorrow morning after we sleep in past sunrise?" His promise sparks such glee, she gasps, inhaling a piece of the muffin she was devouring. Destrin and I laugh as he pats her on the back and offers her a small sip of ale to help it down. Once she's able to breathe normally again, she begins to say something before being cut off by another scream, this one undoubtedly fueled with terror–and much closer.

"What's going on? That doesn't sound like drunk women anymore..." I say, searching the crowd for someone who might be hurt or in need of help. Destrin hands Annie off to Eydis, who holds onto her as protectively as we would. We scan the crowd together, not seeing anything out of the ordinary.

"Stay near Annie, I'll take a look around." He kisses my forehead and stalks the perimeter of the festival. My instincts are screaming at me that something isn't right, I can't pinpoint what it is though. So I settle into a defensive mindset. Deep breaths, continuously searching, constantly listening. I take a seat back at Eydis' table while continuing to scan the area, trying to look past the few dancing villagers and into the smaller groups of people to make sure everyone is alright.

Annie administers a sharp gasp from Eydis' lap, her face pales and eyes widen in fear. Her back is as straight and rigid as an arrow with eyes harboring nothing but pure terror, "Daddy! They're going to hurt Daddy!"

My dinner instantly spoils in my stomach, and I swallow the bile that follows. I never ignore Annie's "feelings." Especially not when this one is so specific—not vague like before our trip to Skogby.

"Hold onto her, keep her safe!" Jumping up from my seat, I hand Eydis a dagger that I have kept strapped to my leg ever since Skogby and rush toward where I saw Destrin last. I pass Pa at a nearby table with his friends, and see him run after me as soon as I pass—sword still strapped to his waist.

"Bree, what's wrong?" He yells behind me, quickly catching up.

"There was screaming and Annie had one of her feelings. It's Destrin, I need to find him."

Like my words signaled them–another scream rises…then another, and another. After mere seconds more than half of the crowd is screaming, but I still can't find the source or my husband. My heart pounds through my chest, ready to escape the confines of flesh and bone if I do not find answers quickly.

A dense fog rolls through the street, making the fire sprites flee from their glass orbs, bringing nothing but darkness, dread, and fear. What was once a warm and comfortable evening moments ago is now conquered by a deep chill in the air, poisoning the atmosphere as the temperature drops significantly. The entire area is only lit by what the moonlight allows. My breathing quickens to match the slamming of my heart, and my head begins to spin. I'm about to turn around to go back to my daughter to rush her home—until I spot them.

Destrin points his sword toward five creatures that could have only been made from the trickster God himself, Loki. These creatures were once men, their skin now gray and sunken in, completely decomposed in large sections—leaving their blackened bones and desiccated organs visible, even in the darkness. Three undead have matted hair and beards, insects weave their way through the coarse strands and locks. Their eyes glow a piercing, unnatural ice blue and their lips have receded completely, showing nothing but their rotted, onyx teeth.

Their leather armor is weathered and torn, looking as if it has been underground for years. Each one carries old battered weapons–swords and axes that are consumed by rust. The smell emanating from them is putrid—decayed human flesh, masking the scent of dark magic in the air.

The one in the front, closest to Destrin, lifts a greatsword above its head and drops its jaw. The mandible falls to its chest with a sickening crack—holding onto the skull by a thin strip of deteriorated flesh. The most horrific sound I've ever heard erupts from its broken face, it erases any sense of courage and hope I had left–replacing it with such horror that my blood runs ice cold, my organs shrivel to nothing, and my brain quakes in my skull. It screeches at such a high pitch that everyone nearby has to cover their ears while it brings tears to our eyes.

The torture stops as abruptly as it began. Silence permeates the air, no one moves or even breathes. All sound in the village has completely vanished as this creature stares at my husband. The rotting men are eerily still, not even swayed by the forceful wind that pushes through the air.

A war cry arises from behind me and gains the horde's attention. They look at the man who runs toward them, and as he passes I see that man is Pa. Sword in hand, my sixty-two year old grandfather rushes toward the danger with a warrior's confidence. Des responds in kind, driving his sword directly through the heart of the monster before him. Its head snaps back to him, and it grabs the blade with its bony hand, forcing it out from its chest until the sword falls with a dull thud onto the ground.

"They're Draugr, Svanhild, you know how to kill 'em so do it!" Pa shouts as he swings his own sword across the neck of a draugr, almost completely decapitating it. Its head swings, dangling against its back and it growls ferociously. Thick black blood like curdled milk slowly spills from the open wound, making the stench around us stronger, more nauseating. Everyone fights this evil with scrunched noses and green faces.

"Oh, I figured I would distract them until you could take care of it, old man! Gotta keep you in shape after all these years. I just want to make sure you still know how to fight!" Destrin jests.

"I'm sure that's all it is. Yet here I am, worried you forgot everythin' from yer days at war!" As Pa jokes, one of the draugr slices his arm with the tip of a spear. He hisses in pain as blood pours down his arm. He lunges forward, pushing his sword into its chest and lifting up, slicing through its torso and head. The rusty spear falls to the ground alongside the body, and Pa continues to the next one.

Someone bumps into my arm as they run past me, heading for another horde of draugr emerging from the trees. The sight brings me back to my senses, I can't just stand here and do nothing. I don't have a weapon, and even if I did, I lost any warrior sense that Destrin and Pa have drilled into me. All of my training has been blown into smoke. All sense chased from my body with the deafening wail.

I run toward the emptying market and immediately look for Eydis and Annie. As I push through the onlooking crowd, I start ushering them all to safety. "Everyone get inside, lock your doors and grab something to use as a weapon!"

Everyone I encounter follows my lead without question, and the instruction leads to Eydis sneaking out from behind a large barrel with Annie held tightly in her arms.

"Mommy, where is Daddy? They're going to hurt him!" Annie cries and reaches her arms toward me.

"I need you to stay with Eydis for now my love, I'll bring you home and then help Daddy, I promise." I take the dagger back from Eydis and begin leading them to the cottages.

Many of the villagers have now gone inside with the exception of a group of men who have come back out with axes and hammers to help my family fight the draugr. We start running as more of the rotting undead come from the forest surrounding the outer part of the market. The village will soon be completely overrun by these creatures unless we can kill them off. Eydis and I make it far enough down the road that we are halfway home, just a couple more minutes before we reach safety—when we skid to a stop, nearly toppling over each other as my eyes lock onto the milky pools of another. The largest draugr of the group steps out of the dark, directly in our path.

My heart drops into my stomach, and my clammy hands almost lose hold of my dagger. The draugr is easily taller than my husband and braces a spear taller than myself. It stands so close that the stench from its flesh assaults my senses, and the fog that creeps behind it has completely surrounded us. The most terrifying bit of it all is that he doesn't look at me, but directly at my daughter-cowering in Eydis' embrace.

The massive draugr lifts its spear—pointing it directly at my baby.
And throws it.

SEVEN
BREE

No.

No, no, no!

I fall to my knees as my husband collides into my arms. Shock widening his eyes that frantically look for mine, and as he finds them I feel like I can see his life flashing before him.

He's been dealt a death blow—this is his end.

Pa is shouting and metal collides with surrounding draugr before everything becomes completely muffled. The only thing I can hear clearly is Destrin's rattled breaths. I know I should ensure we are protected, but I can't tear my eyes from him—I can't break this connection when it could be all I have left. I can't look at anything else besides my husband who jumped in front of a spear to save our daughter. Annie pushes up against me, and I know that Pa protects us. That is enough for me at this moment.

I lay his head upon my left forearm and place my right hand on his chest, willing it to never stop the rise and fall that means he lives. The long spear protrudes from his chest, and by the sound of his breathing, it has punctured a lung. Blood slowly pulses from the edges of the wound and his breaths are loud and strained—fighting against the blood that creeps into his throat. My hands are covered with it, and I'm hit with the impossible reality that there will be no saving my husband.

"No, Des, you can't leave me, you can't leave us. We need you, we need you my love, please please please!" My pleas fade off into a whisper, begging the Gods to let this be a dream—a nightmare—anything but reality. I cannot stop the sobs that wrack my chest, rivers cascade down my cheeks and onto the blood-matted hair against his neck. My head falls onto his shoulder, and I soak in the warmth that still embraces his skin.

This can't be real.

I can't lose him.

I can't do the coming journey without this man by my side. My soulmate, my love, my best friend. Ripped away from me as Nan was. I cry into his hair and cradle him, holding him as close as I possibly can to my heart. A heart that is shattering to dust.

The man who can make me laugh on the gloomiest of days, the one who I tell everything that runs through my mind. Who always picks me up when I fall only to remind me that it's a small misstep, that everything will be okay.

But it won't be okay, not this time. Not with Destrin gone.

"Wife...love." Blood sputters onto the corners of his lips as he tries to speak.

I move to look at his face once again, clearing my tears with the hand not holding him so that I can see him clearly.

"Sword..." he whispers.

Sword...he needs me to make sure his weapon is in his hand before he's gone. I reach over to his arm and notice he still grips the hilt of his magnificent sword, albeit weakly. "It's okay love, you have it, you will drink with the Gods soon enough." I force a shaky smile to comfort him as a fresh set of tears soaks my face. With such tragedy, I have to cling to the knowledge that he will soon be feasting and drinking to his heart's content–with warriors past, and Gods alike.

His arm that is closest to me raises with a bloodied hand to hold my face. And with his eyes he tells me all of the words he cannot speak.

The pure passion and love in his gaze is enough to tell me everything that he says to me every day. He has never let me forget how much he loves me. The corners of his lips slant downward slightly, and his brow settles into hard determination. "Ann...Annie."

Annie hears her father's words, and she rushes to Destrin's opposite side, looking down at his sword in hand. His grip has slipped, and noticing this, she wraps her small hands around his fingers, gigantic in comparison, so that he is holding his weapon once again.

"Daddy, I love you." She says in a small whimper. He looks at her with such pride and unconditional love–a love untouchable by those who have never experienced a relationship like theirs.

Although love cannot adequately describe the emotion that sings from his soul when he looks at her. When it comes to our child, no words have yet been created to properly explain the pure radiance that warms our chests when we look at her. A smile spreads across his beautiful face as he takes us both in one last time. He can barely get any noise from his chest, but manages a soft few words, "My girls...will see...again...love...you."

With his final breath, his gaze turns to the sky. The sky that just hours ago was a beautiful blue, hosted the shining sun, and the softest of breezes. The sky is now filled with thousands of stars, gazing upon the bloody scene that is our village–my world. The sky where he will travel with the Valkyrie to the land of the Gods and be honored with a warrior's death.

Annie sobs as her head falls to his shoulder, still ensuring that his hand grips his sword as tightly as she possibly can. I lean forward and press my lips against my husband's one final time, soaking in the lingering warmth, and memorizing the feeling. For it will be all I have for the rest of my mortal life.

BEST BY FAR

The day mocks me.

The sun dominates the sky, not a single cloud daring to dull its shine. It sparkles across the sea, so calm it looks like glass. The temperature is perfect for kids to play outside and for the market to thrive with the life of our village. Yet, despite the beauty of the day, neither occurs.

Today we honor my husband with his funeral pyre—a week after his sacrifice—and I cannot stand the thought of it. We shouldn't be doing this for another 60 years, but the draugr needlessly claimed his life and tore my family apart.

Pa leaves his cottage and stands beside me, underneath my favorite maple tree. "Is Annie almost ready?" He implores in a low, soft tone.

"She was eating breakfast when I came outside. She's dressed and will be ready." I say, my voice monotone with indifference.

As if she heard us, Annie comes outside. Her clothes mirror mine, a black dress with a woven leather belt around the waist. Our hair is braided into the same intricate patterns, leaving half of it down to dance with the wind. I have painted a rune for luck and protection onto our foreheads. She walks over to us in her worn brown slippers and says nothing as she wraps her arms around my waist and rests her cheek on my hip. We look out upon the sea together and I run my fingers through the part of her hair that flows down her back.

"Where will we put Daddy's ashes after the funeral?" She asks with a sniffle from her running nose.

"Where do you wish to lay them, little love?"

"I think we should give him to the sea…then he can go anywhere he wants and we can visit him on our beach."

"I love that, Annie. It's a beautiful idea and he would love it." I lower myself to the ground and embrace her. Her little arms wrap themselves around my neck and we stay there, holding onto each other as we prepare to say goodbye to the most important man in both of our lives.

Pa watches over us and places his hands on our shoulders for comfort. I give him one of my hands in response—grateful that he survived the fight.

Destrin was the only casualty that night. All of the other men, including Pa, obtained various injuries but ultimately came through.

Destrin died because I'm weak...

I shudder and close my eyes tightly, forcing a few tears to fall from my lashes as I squeeze Pa's hand. Annie hears the small whimper that escapes me and pulls away, looking into my eyes and wiping my tears.

I smile at my beautiful girl, eyes brimming with her own silent tears. "Thank you, little love. We will always help each other when we're down. We'll miss Daddy so much, every day. But as the days go on we'll learn how to live in his absence and we'll keep his memory alive." Nodding her head in agreement, she pulls out the Ouroboros armband from her dress pocket that once belonged to Des. As she holds it in the sunlight, we watch the gold shine across the intricate designs along the serpent's scales and head. It was made to resemble the World Serpent, Jörmungandr.

"Keep that close to you, Annie. It means a great deal for someone to receive such a gift, and it will protect you in the future." Pa tells her, stepping away from us. "I'll go on ahead and meet you at the pyre, take your time here."

We stay there for a few moments, looking at this last piece of Destrin and settling in the comfort of each other. I summon Mead, and he immediately rubs his head against Annie's legs, trying to provide any extra love he can manage.

"I'm ready Mama. Are you?"

"I will never be ready to say goodbye, my love. But I will be as strong as you are and do what I must." I stand, taking her free hand in mine. We begin the walk toward the far beaches where the village has built the funeral pyre for my husband, large enough for him to make his journey to Valhalla with ease.

The pyre stands nearly as tall as the trees in the forest, a sign of great respect. Destrin was a beloved member of our community, always helping others and available when he was needed. After his efforts and sacrifice during the attack, the villagers were more than grateful for Destrin's bravery. Eydis came by every day to help look after Annie. Every day she came, she brought with her another story of that night, from someone Destrin saved while fighting the onslaught of the undead.

One of the children lost her parents in the commotion and was spotted by a roaming draugr. Destrin grabbed her and ran toward one of the shops, tossing her inside the open window to the people hiding inside. He took an arrow in the back while covering an elderly couple who hadn't been able to move quickly enough. He must have pulled it out before he jumped in front of Annie.

He shouldn't have had to do that, I failed him and my daughter...

He flipped multiple tables onto their sides for people to hide behind.

I helped no one but myself.

He killed at least fourteen draugr on his own.

And I did nothing but stare and run.

He saved at least ten villagers from a gruesome fate.

Yet I couldn't save him from his.

He's a hero and an honored warrior.

I'm nothing but a weak, scared woman.

"Bree, get out of your head, I can practically hear yer thoughts from here" I hadn't noticed Pa until now, looking over the pyre beside me.

I turn my head toward him and give the best smile I can muster. It probably resembles more of a grimace than a smile, but he understands.

Redirecting the subject away from my self deprecation, I glance at my husband's body lying delicately upon the wood. "I'm very grateful for what the village has done for us this last week. This pyre is beautiful, there's no doubt the smoke will rise directly to Valhalla to guide him." I hardly recognize my own voice, but it reflects the aching numbness throughout my heart.

"There's no doubt he would be brought there anyway, Bree. He was one Hel of a man. The Gods simply wanted to feast with him sooner."

They knew I didn't deserve him, that's why they took him from me.

"Well, I wish they could have at least let Annie have a father for a little bit longer. And I, my husband." My words spit more venom than a snake, allowing my anger at the Gods to show more than I would like.

The villagers begin to form a circle around the pyre. Four men come forward with lit torches and stand in each corner of the rectangular pyre, ready for the signal to set it aflame. Annie and I move forward toward Destrin's best friend, Leif, who came home early from a hunting trip after receiving word of the attack. He nods to me in greeting and hands me a ceremonial bow and arrow.

The villagers are completely silent out of respect for Des. A few move aside, and Jarl Borgsik approaches, lit torch in hand. The same thin, blonde woman follows closely behind with another round of pints like she did just last week. As she hands them out, the Jarl stands directly before Annie and I, a solemn smile paints his face.

"I've met your husband quite a few times, Ms. Ragna. He was a proud warrior and a respectable man. One of those times, he was dining with myself and his fellow soldiers. We spoke of what it would be like to die in battle and what we hope for afterwards. I distinctly remember his answer, as I think everyone who attended will, 'I would expect nothing less than for my loved ones to drink to my life and drink again to my death, then once more because ale is delicious!'" The crowd laughs around us, victims to Destrin's humor even when he's gone. A small laugh surprises me as I can easily imagine my husband saying those exact words. The pint woman approaches, and the Jarl hands me one himself, "So I have supplied the ale, and we will do just that."

"Thank you, Jarl Borgsik. Your generosity means the world to us."

He takes his stance behind me and my daughter, handing us the reins to begin the ceremony. Stepping forward so that I stand out amongst the circle of mourners, I lose control of the tears that I've been fighting thus far. I blame the Jarl's story and of his thoughtfulness to do this for Des. Him attending the ceremony personally tells much about my husband.

"Good Morn' everyone," I shout to the crowd, forcing my voice to be as strong as I can. "As you all know, my husband was a magnificent man. He took care of his family and friends, he helped most of you at one point or another and always enjoyed it. He was very sarcastic and a jokester in his own right. He was a warrior. A friend. A husband. And a father." My voice breaks at my last words and I am met with sobs I can no longer cage in. Annie sniffles beside me, squeezing my hand. I take a few deep breaths to continue on, channeling her strength to guide me. "He died saving our little girl, and I know he wouldn't have it any other way. Doing something that you know will end your life to save the life of your child is something every parent I know would choose in a heartbeat. I would have chosen it myself if Destrin hadn't been more nimble than I." I look down at Annie and our tears simultaneously track down our cheeks.

"I have never met a more honorable man than him, and we're all lucky to have known him. Thank you all for the work you have put into this day. Thank you for being a part of my husband's life, and thank you for the selflessness you have shown my family. So now, before we light the pyre, I would like us all to raise our pints, in honor of Destrin Svanhild." I give my full attention to the man who lays before me, " I now make a final promise to you, husband. One day, I will follow you across the Nine Realms and into eternity. For now though, I'll drink to your legacy."

Everyone raises their arms in solidarity, pints high in the air. I take a swig, and give Leif the rest of the pint as I raise my bow and notch the arrow, signaling him to light the head. I aim my arrow at the wood beneath Des, stealing one last glance at him.

Before my eyes can be blurred by my tears, I let the arrow loose. The middle of the pyre ignites rapidly and the men standing in each corner set more flames to the spots in front of them. All at once, the skies are filled with the shouts of men and women who are mourning and memorializing Destrin. May he feast with the Gods, and protect us in our coming journey.

Skål.

EIGHT
BREE

Pa and I walk back to the cottages with Annie asleep in my arms, her head resting heavily on my shoulder. Each step I take brings me closer to a world without Destrin. A place where his essence resides around every corner, but he himself is nowhere to be found. I'm not ready to live in that world, I shouldn't have had to for another sixty plus years. Annie should be able to grow up with her father teaching her how to fight and survive outside the village. She should have a mother teaching her how to be strong and resilient. For the foreseeable future, I'm not sure I can be either of those things for her.

The closer we get to our home, my chest tightens, and nausea creeps higher into my throat. My limbs quickly become weaker, each step an unbearable challenge. Pa notices my pace slowing and turns to me, trying to read my facial expression.

"It's okay, Bree. I can take her home and lay her down in bed if yer not ready to go back inside yet," Pa offers gently.

I take a deep breath through my nose and slowly let it out. As I close my eyes, I try to focus on anything but the darkness that shadows my mind. After a moment, I look at my grandfather and give a reassuring smile.

"Thank you, but I must face it and get the initial torture of the ghost of him over with. I also don't want Annie to wake up to neither of her parents, she needn't be traumatized any further."

Approaching my home, I imagine laying Annie down, and throwing on one of Destrin's tunics to join her for a much needed nap. I used to hate those tunics. They have the sleeves cut off, and the holes are huge on my smaller frame and very revealing, but they were his favorite, and I bet I can find one that still smells like him.

Before we're able to make it any closer, the air shifts.

Something is wrong.

The area feels dark, cold, and disrespected.

Pa glances at me as he says, "Stay here with Annie, I'll check everything to make sure no one is here."

He lowers his stance, walking silently toward the stone pathways while bent forward and arms out in front of him ready for an attack. While he checks the houses, I scour the surrounding trees. I don't see anything out of place or any misplaced shadows.

"Mead, come help sweet boy." The black cat appears between my feet and after rubbing against my legs, he trots into our yard, helping in the search for the darkening presence.

I take small steps around the perimeter, my arms keeping Annie in a protective embrace. My eyes continue to scan the area and they land on the stump where Des used to chop wood. There's something sticking where his axe used to be, and it's the only thing that could explain the tension in the air. As I approach the stump, the object comes into clear view and I stop in my tracks.

"Pa!" I can't help the fear that laces my voice.

"What did you find?" He yells, jogging over to me, his breathing labored. He follows my gaze until he spots a knife wrapped in twine sticking out of the stump.

"I take it this isn't yours or Destrin's?" He reaches down to pull it out of the wood and looks at it closely. As he studies it, my legs begin to buckle and my entire body trembles.

"When we were in Skogby," I stutter, "The fisherman who trapped Mead had *that* knife. He was twirling it around his fingers at The Angler's Cove. He—he was here...he clearly has some kind of dark magic. What if he sent the draugr? This cannot be a coincidence, this is a threat." The longer I speak, the weaker my voice grows until it breaks at the name of the creature who killed the love of my life.

Tears silently drift down my cheeks and I can barely manage a whisper. "The draugr was aiming for Annie...the youngest Asvaldan heir. They were sent to kill the heirs...they know about Annie."

My realization of the true culprit forges my grief into rage. Those monsters were meant to end the Asvaldan bloodline, yet because of my husband's sacrifice, they failed. I turn to face Pa and when I meet his gaze, I'm met with familiar rage.

Nan.

"This is the end of him. He has pushed our family too far. It's time we avenge Nan, and the memory of Destrin will guide us to the end. It's time we bring him our vengeance, wouldn't you agree Pa?"

He nods his head once. "Aye. The man has reigned long enough and has taken too much."

"Yes, he has."

We both turn to rest Annie gently on a wooden bench on our porch. Once she's settled I meet Pa's determined gaze–shining brightly as inspiration grows between the two of us.

"He's had the throne in his power and our family has been hiding in an imaginary bubble of safety for far too long. He will no longer kill us off one by one. It's time the Asvaldan's were back on the throne, where Nan belonged. I'll make sure we take back her birthright and do right by our family."

I search the sea where the sun glimmers off the soft waves, looking elegant and peaceful in more mockery of me. Pa can probably hear the wheels spinning in my head. Determination plants inside my heart, possible plans to end the Regent swirling into a storm.

"We'll need support, warriors, and power in order to accomplish this. Simply going in and assassinating the man will do nothing but make us appear treasonous. The people would kill me and ask questions later—I won't have the chance to explain who I really am."

"Even if ya did have the chance, the only people who would hear ya are men loyal to him. They would either kill ya before you could tell the public, or spin tales so no one would believe you to begin with. Yer blood is yer biggest strength in this war."

Pa is right, I will need to create a perfect plan in order to pull this off. We must end with the Asvalda's back in power, the people behind us, and the Regent dead.

"I can't leave without Annie, and she's too young and fragile for this journey. We'll take the years leading up to her eighteenth birthday to hone my magic further, and we'll both learn how to fight on the battlefield."

Learning how to use my magic more efficiently and training won't be enough. Having an army behind me will help but it won't secure his demise. He cannot simply be human with the power he radiates. To still be alive this long without aging a day since usurping the throne. We've seen proof of the dark magic that he wields in his henchman and creatures. I need a weapon that an evil such as himself cannot stand against.

"Yer Uncle Jaris is Jarl of Frostheim in the mountain lands. He's been a hidden pawn by the Regent's side for his whole career, he will have somewhere fer ya' to start planning. He's been preparin' his whole life to be of help to our girls when the time comes. Jaris is the True Queen's son after all. He may not have a claim to the throne for being male, but he has her blood—yer blood, and that's undeniable."

I haven't seen my Uncle Jaris in almost ten years, but he was always happy to see and play with me when I was a child. We still correspond by letter every year. He's the perfect asset to gain allies and information to begin playing the most popular game in nobility.

Attaining power.

PART TWO

NINE
ANNIE

The cool touch of the sea surrounding Gledibyr embraces my feet, sending a shock to my senses and goosebumps to rise along my legs. Since I was five years old, I've come to the beach by my cottage every morning to say hello to my father. When the ashes of the honored Destrin Svanhild were given to my family, we let them be carried by the wind out to sea so that he could wander the world. I don't think he wanders too far though, I can feel his presence with me every time I come to the beach where we released him.

He used to play with me on this shore any time I asked, and I remember always laughing on the way home because we were always covered in sand, and knew Mother would hate the mess. He taught me to face my fears of the water when I was terrified of something pulling me under.

"Nothing will pull you under, little love. And if something does, punch it right in the nose, and it will give you right back!" He laughed and ran his hand over the top of my auburn hair.

"So if I punch you in the nose, will you let go while I run to the sweets cabinet?" I asked with my hands on my hips and gave him a competitive look. He threw his head back and let out a booming laugh, running his hand across his face and over his stubbly beard.

"Absolutely not, and now that I know your plan, I'll make sure not to be at your eye level anymore, you little demon child."

He would let me pretend to help him and Pa when they would go fishing out on the canoe, giving me a child-size pole of my own where I caught all kinds of fish. He taught me to be proud of myself and to be happy with what I can accomplish. I later learned that he was tossing his catches toward my pole when he threw them back in, and that's how I managed to catch a decent amount of them, but learning that trick of his made me appreciate him even more.

He was beginning to teach me a dance of swords with a wooden practice sword Pa made for me. Once my father was gone, Pa took up the responsibility and helped my mother with her training as well. I can still hear my father's roaring laughter when I would say something witty to him or my mother, the way he would sneak me a wink she wouldn't see.

I can feel the safety of his embrace when I would have nightmares, and when he reassured me that nothing bad would get me. I can still smell the freshly chopped wood mixed with pine that made up his scent. Mother and I split up some of his shirts when we were adjusting to our new life without him, so we could smell him for a bit longer until it wore off.

I miss him every day.

As I stare across the gentle waves that glitter in the morning sunrise, I place my hand around the golden arm ring on my wrist. I'll be forever grateful he gave me his Ouroboros before he died. It brings me comfort when I feel the weight of it, and I've noticed the small smile that wishes to spread across my mother's face every time she looks at it. The Ouroboros ring was the best gift he could have given me for the coming journey he didn't foresee, but the Norns had planned.

As for the Norn's plan, tomorrow is my eighteenth birthday, and I'll finally have magic at my disposal. Mother and Pa have been teaching me everything they know over the last few years in preparation for this. All of the times I've caught my mother and Pa huddled together in hushed whispers, witnessed her read letters on foreign stationary in secret, and the cryptic riddles in regard to my future—it will all be answered tomorrow.

I take a deep breath, slowly letting it escape my lips, and say a silent goodbye to Father. Lost in watching my steps through the sand, I head back up the beach to help Mother get ready for tomorrow. She has planned a huge celebration for my birthday and has invited the entire village to join the festivities.

As I approach our cottage, I catch a glimpse of her walking back and forth past the kitchen window, finishing up some food that will be served tomorrow. Once I'm through the front door, I notice about thirty thin ropes draped across the dining room table and a large crate of clear, empty bulbs with wide openings for the fire sprites.

"Annie! I'm putting the lights together for the market, can you start tying the bulbs to the ropes? I need to go talk to the fire sprites and make sure we have everything they want for tomorrow's feast."

I adore the sprites. They are joyous, happy creatures and never fail to make me smile. "Of course, but can I come with you to see the sprites? I haven't seen them in ages and I've never seen where they live."

She freezes mid step, almost as if she's re-evaluating her plans to incorporate me. Her dark brown hair is pulled back into a messy braid that has already begun falling apart. She has slight lines between her eyes as she processes her thoughts, and a light sheen of sweat across her forehead. I wonder when she began working her tail off this morning, I really should try to reel her in for a break at some point.

"I think we can arrange that. We just need to be quick in order to get this done in time. I would ask Pa to work on it while we're gone but his hands have been bothering him lately." As she speaks, she grabs an old canvas shoulder bag hanging on a hook by the door. She fills it with bottles of mead and some of the bread she baked last night. "Alright, ready to go?"

A huge grin overwhelms my face, I love talking to the fire sprites, "Absolutely!"

With her bag slung across her chest and a quick wave towards Pa's cottage, we're off to deliver some mead. The fire sprites have fascinated me for as long as I can remember. From what I've been told, the people of Gledibyr have always had a great relationship with them. They're fun, free-spirited little creatures and always seem to have a good time. They love helping us with nighttime events like feasts and festivals. They say it is just as fun for them as it is for us—it also gives us much better lighting than lit torches scattered around the square.

"Annie, I'm glad we have this chance together. I have some news that you need to hear. It will come as a shock, I'm sure. But I'm here to answer any of your questions and you must know before tomorrow."

A million possibilities rush through my head. I assume this is in regard to the journey we'll be leaving for in the coming weeks. But with a glance, I spot her wringing her hands together nervously, and she is biting her lip, waiting for my response.

"What is it?" I ask gently, almost whispering. After taking a deep, controlled breath, she straightens her stance, lifting her chin slightly like she has been anxiously preparing herself for this moment.

"You know of the Regent," she begins. I nod and urge her to continue. "He has a history of tearing families apart and bending our Kingdom to his every whim." As she speaks, she continues staring off into the distance ahead of us. "When Nan was young, the Regent murdered her family. Not liking to leave survivors, he made it his mission to find her after she fled his grasp. Obviously, she got away and came here where she restarted her life."

"But he found her eventually—in Skogby," I interrupt.

"He did."

For a few moments we walked in silence. I kick a small stone repeatedly, granting Mother a chance to gather her thoughts. She hasn't shown emotion thus far, but her jaw is noticeably tense.

"The story goes much deeper than I can let on currently, but our journey has much to do with Nan's history. Who she was defines our lives on a level most could never even dream of. I promise to give you more answers soon, but since you may hear things during our errand today, I felt it necessary to clue you in to some extent. A war will come, little one, and I have been preparing for it for most of your life."

Small glowing orbs of fire completely surround me, most are the size of a plump strawberry. Some are dancing from tree to tree, spiraling between the branches before flying to another. Others are sitting around in circles, vibrating in excitement. Once we approach them, I can distinguish more than just their flames. I can see their smiles, hear their laughter, and notice that the flames on top of their heads is actually hair.

After a few of them notice my mother approaching, they go silent. One by one, hundreds of tiny figures turn to face us with looks of awe. They must be the ones who know why humans come to them, to offer them mead and bread. After a few silent moments, I start to feel like we have interrupted something important and aren't as welcome as I imagined we would be. Right as I reach out to grab mother's sleeve, rustling starts behind a large tree a little further away.

A blue light appears from the tree. Once fully emerged, I notice this one has the same features as the other fire sprites, but is larger—about the size of a pear. I've never seen a blue fire sprite before, I wonder if there are more of them?

"Bree Ragna. It has been too long, my dear friend." The sprite has a peaceful countenance as she gazes at my mother, speaking in a serene, melodic voice. They walk forward to one another and the sprite touches my mother's outstretched fingers in greeting.

"It has, and I apologize for not finding more time to visit you, Nuri." My mother bows her head slightly.

"I understand. I'm sure your preparations have been taking up much of your time. When do you plan to begin?"

Has my mother been planning my birthday for so long that it has hindered her time to see someone who she's clearly close with? That can't be right. She just started her typical panicking this past week to make sure everything is perfect. Before that, she seemed to have plenty of time to see her friends. The only other thing she's been doing is practicing her magic and fighting skills a little bit more, but she's always been on top of everything.

Mother lowers her head close to Nuri's ear and whispers something I can't make out. With a quick glance in my direction, I notice a flash of shock as she looks at me before her features soften once more. As they part, their eyes remain on me, igniting a spark of annoyance.

"Does this have to do with my birthday?" I question, a hint of irritation in my voice.

Sensing my confusion, four fire sprites climb onto me. One on each shoulder, one holding my hand, and the last two spinning in perfect pirouettes on my feet.

"Why isn't my clothing or hair burning with them on me?" Their distraction softens my ire.

"Because we're able to control our heat. If we do not wish to burn someone or something then we can suppress our flames. That's how we are able to live freely in the forest." Nuri says wistfully. "And yes, your mother did mention something regarding your coming journey. You will find out soon enough, sweet girl. In order to protect you, this secret had to be kept between as few people as possible and unfortunately, a child isn't always capable of such secrets."

"I understand that, but feeling so left in the dark while others have more intel on me isn't something I particularly enjoy."

Mother separates from Nuri and stands beside me, taking my hands in hers and replacing the small sprite. She looks into my eyes with a gentle expression. "Annie...there are things that have been hidden within our family for longer than you and I have been alive. Secrets that have been put into place in order to protect not only our family, but the entire kingdom of Asvalda. I know I confused you with the small snippet of information on the way here; I need you to know that there is importance in this visit besides confirming party plans. Can you trust me to fill you in soon—with Pa's help?"

I contemplate my mother's words carefully, wanting more information, but realizing she wouldn't keep anything from me without a good reason. "Of course I trust you, I'm just confused and to be honest, and a little nervous because of the secrecy."

"I know, little love. Soon you will know absolutely everything, I assure you." She braces herself on the mossy ground as she stands, turning back toward Nuri. The large fire sprite moves to a root protruding from a mound of soil, high enough off the ground to now be level with mother's face. "Nuri, I have come to finalize the plans for the feast tomorrow, but I also have a second, much larger request I must make of you. I hope that as a dear friend and citizen of Asvalda, you will think on this request carefully."

I can count on one hand the number of times I've seen my mother look as apprehensive as she seems at this moment. She takes a deep breath, lifting her chin ever so slightly while maintaining eye contact with Nuri.

"I believe I know what you will be asking, Bree, spit it out my dear."

A small chuckle escapes her, visibly lessening her nerves. Mother places both hands in front of her, resting against her stomach. "In two short days, our fates will come to fruition. The journey will not be a short one, and I can't anticipate how many moon cycles will pass before we fulfill our task. When it comes to the end—when it is time to avenge my family, I need Asvalda behind me. I am requesting all of the help that I can possibly require and—"

"Bree Ragna, I do not burn blue for no reason at all. I have been given my enhanced powers by the Gods because I will always do what it takes to protect my people and the land that has been so gracious to us—the friends who have always been there for us."

A small breeze, that's most certainly magic, gently pushes Nuri closer to my mother, "When the time comes, the fire sprites will stand behind you and help until the very end."

With a single, silent tear cascading down Mother's cheek, it hits me. The war she mentioned is not a dramatic inspiration. We're about to walk into an incredibly dangerous future. It's a blessing that I am the product of Destrin Svanhild and Bree Ragna because I believe that I have been unknowingly preparing for this my entire life.

TEN
BREE

The walk home from visiting Nuri is quiet, but luckily, it doesn't feel awkward. I know my daughter trusts me and my intentions. I continuously glance at her to try to see if she looks more frustrated rather than contemplative. I can't tell for sure.

When we arrive home, she seems anxious to see Pa. She won't let our secrecy go on a moment longer, and I can't say I blame her. While they sit at our dining room table, I walk over to the fireplace to stoke the surviving flame and boil some water for tea.

Pa has always been a good story teller, it is one of the many things the old man is known for. In order for Annie to comprehend our lineage and past, he's the best person to share our history and details. He's sitting at the head of the table with Annie to his left, and he takes her hand in his. With a nervous look toward me, I nod my head for him to begin.

"My dear little Annie. There's so much for us to teach you, about who you really are, and where you come from. I wish your great-grandmother was here to tell you herself, because this all started with her." He stands and walks down the hall to his bedroom, coming back with a sketch of a beautiful woman who looks around my age. "This is Nan, as you know. Here in Gledibyr, she went by Cyn Ragna. Mother of two, and wife of a blacksmith. But in the city of Valderra, 55 years ago, she was Princess Correa Asvalda, heir to the kingdom of Asvalda."

"Nan was...a princess? *The* Princess? How did she end up here?" For a moment, I see my sweet five year old girl, in awe of the fairytales we told her to sleep.

"I'm getting to that, young one." He falls quiet and silently looks at the sketch that he drew of his wife when they were young and in love.

"Cyn's parents were the King and Queen. No one knows much about the man we call the Regent, but we do know that he greatly coveted the power given to the Asvaldan bloodline by the Gods a thousand years ago. This power only flows through the female line, which is why my son Jaris lives in the mountains, wantin' to make his own future worthy of his Ma's blood."

"Does the Regent know who Uncle Jaris really is?" Annie asks, her eyes as large as apples in amazement.

"I don't suspect he does. Jaris has worked hard to keep his true self and our family a secret. He joined the military as soon as he turned yer age so he could keep an army close at hand if—when his Ma needed it. When Nan had no intention of wagin' a war, he started to make plans with Tessa, your grandmother. Anyway, the Regent gathered a force that was small enough not to be noticed right away, but large enough to overthrow the monarchs, taking the throne for himself. Cyn's Mother's last words were to go into hiding, gather forces throughout the kingdom, and take back the throne. Instead, she fled to Skogby and met a handsome young lad who swept her off her feet and she never looked back."

Annie quickly turns in her chair to face me as I place three porcelain mugs onto the table, and pour us each a cup of tea. Her jaw is halfway to the table in awe and she has a hint of confusion in her eyes. "Why did Nan never go back for the throne?"

"Well, from my understanding, once she met Pa she realized that she had no idea of how to help her people. The best thing that she could possibly do at that time was keep herself safe, create some heirs, and make sure the Regent never ended the Asvaldan line," I tell her softly, taking my turn to admire my grandmother's beautiful features in the frame. She's where Annie inherited the beautiful auburn hair and light green eyes, light freckles dancing across both of their cheeks.

"If the Regent already sits upon the throne then why must he be so set on killing us off?"

"The way the magic of the Gods works is when they bless a family of their choosing to rule a kingdom, that family is granted a fraction of the magic they possess. The same magic that you'll be able to wield after tomorrow, when you come of age. This magic can only be passed along to the female heirs, not to other family members or usurpers, like the Regent, unless he kills all of the heirs. He will only ever be the true ruler of the realm if we're all dead."

I pass Nan's picture back to Pa and look at my daughter solemnly as I prepare to explain the rest of the story. "Nan was killed by the Regent. That's how he realized she had heirs, because the power of the Gods did not yet flow in his veins. Nan created a barrier around this island to protect herself, it stopped him from being able to find her. It's a risk when any of us leave, although my mother had put a small spell of her own over our family to protect us further. Pa and I believe that Nan's protection may have weakened after her passing, allowing evil to come here and find us."

"They found us? Then how are we still here? Still alive...how come they didn't come to finish us off?"

"They did find us." I pause to compose myself, not allowing the agony clawing in my chest to break through and possess me. After a few deep breaths I clear my throat and fidget with the silver ring on my left hand. "They found us thirteen years ago."

Her entire body tenses, putting together the timeline.

"Your father and I went to Skogby to investigate some rumors we heard that may have been about Tessa. While we were there, there was a fisherman who stalked us and trapped Mead in a circle of fire. He knew who I was, that I was inside of Mead's mind, and he stood outside of the window where we slept."

An image of wet alleyways and the sound of twigs breaking underfoot flashes before me. Fire circles around my vision, pulling me into the memory. A soft push against my shin tells me I summoned Mead while my worry from that night makes a re-appearance.

"I remember you going on that trip, I begged you not to because I felt something bad was going to happen. That is when Samuel and the others drowned…"

I look over at the part of the table beneath my mug, moving it over slightly so I can touch the imperfection in the wood. I focus on the memory of how it got there, rather than my fear of what happened in Skogby.

Destrin had attempted to play a foolish game he learned at the pub, stabbing a dagger in between his fingers that were splayed across the table, steadily increasing his speed. In his cockiness, he nicked his thumb, forcing the blade he used into the table. My fingers trace the gash before the image of a twine wrapped knife protruding from a stump outside takes over. My breath hitches in surprise at the intrusion, so I press on, "Do you remember the next time you experienced that feeling?"

Tears begin to pool in her round eyes and she lifts her hand to cover her mouth as she puts together the pieces I laid before her. "Are you telling me that the Regent was behind father's death as well?" Her voice breaks.

I lose the battle against my own tears. "Yes Annie. The fisherman followed us home and sent the draugr to the village to kill us. Destrin saved us all, and his death was his sacrifice for you and this kingdom."

The cottage becomes unnaturally still. The only sound to be heard is Annie's sniffling and Pa's boot, tapping quickly beneath the table.

"He was a good man, yer dad," he says.

I become hyper aware of the sunlight flooding into the room, showcasing layers of dust in each corner that I've neglected for years. Speaking of Des' death again makes me realize how gone he really is.

Wood for the hearth is stacked neatly next to it—Des would have it messily piled in the corner of the room. The heat from the hearth closes in around me, choking me in my misery. It's nothing like the cozy embrace it used to remind me of when my husband was here. The lack of him breaks me, but his sacrifice drives me.

Today was incredibly long and emotionally draining. As I lay in bed thinking over how the talk with Annie went, I can't help the ache in my chest that has plagued me whenever I think of Des. If he were here now, he would be preparing me for the journey that we embark on in two short days. Annie took the rest of the news particularly well, better than I thought she would. After hours of tossing and turning, I decide to put on my robe and sandals to walk outside and sit by the water to visit my husband, desperate to feel his presence.

Tossing my shoes to the side, I let the cold sand envelope my feet as I sit on the edge of the water so when the tide comes in it just misses my toes.

Looking over the sea, I'm amazed with how beautiful the moon and stars sparkle across the water. While sitting with my knees up and arms wrapped around them, I close my eyes and imagine my husband's handsome face. I picture his long hair, so dark it was practically black. His intense glare he gave everyone but me, his warm embrace and intoxicating grin. If I focus hard enough, I can almost feel him sitting behind me, wrapping his arms around my own and smelling my hair for the almond soap he always loved.

"Des, I wish you were here. You would be so proud of our girl. When being told of the danger of our journey she showed nothing but strength and determination. She strives to help our people and to avenge your death." I grab a handful of sand and slowly let it fall through my fingers. "You should be here. You should be teaching her how to fight, keeping her safe while we travel, and you should be here with me. Safe in bed, holding me as I sleep. I shouldn't have to live without you, we had so many more years ahead of us Des..." The grief of the night takes over, and I willingly give into it.

As I cry with my head between my knees there's a sudden breeze that gently kisses the back of my neck. I place my hand over the spot and look back up at the stars, certain that my husband just tried to comfort me.

Another gentle gust touches my cheek and warmth spreads throughout my chest, feeling as if the wind is wrapping itself around me in an embrace of its own. Fallen leaves nearby begin to dance in the breeze, twirling together towards the water and acting as if they're putting on a performance for their small audience.

"Thank you, my love." I whisper to the night air. "I long for the day I join you in Valhalla, and until then I will celebrate the life you lived, and fight for the life our daughter will live."

ELEVEN

ANNIE

"I'm nervous."

"Don't be nervous, it will come naturally to you by day's end, I promise." Mother replies while she holds her morning tea.

"What if it doesn't like me?"

Her eyes soften, recognizing my fear no matter how silly it is. "Annie, this creature is a part of you. It's simply an extension of you, of course it will like you."

"Mother, with all due respect, I'm also an extension of you and there are times we fight like cats and dogs."

She bursts into laughter, spitting her mouthful of tea and crossing an arm over her stomach.

"Touché, my dear. But this is different, while you're an extension of me by blood, your familiar will be connected to you through your soul directly. It is not just *like* you, it *is* you."

Mead, my mother's familiar, suddenly appears like black mist, twirling his feline body around her ankles and softly mewling. "See, it's nothing. I simply want him here and then he is. I know you don't know what type of creature you'll have just yet, so close your eyes and imagine a ball of light. I want you to—Annie take this seriously. Close your eyes!"

"Sorry this just feels a little silly" I stifle a giggle and close my eyes. "Please continue, I'm picturing the ball of light."

"I want you to place that ball of light right beside you, and reach your hand toward it, let your subconscious take over and you'll know what to do."

As best as I can, I do as instructed and imagine the ball of light directly beside me on the beach. Rather than floating beside me, it glides down to the sand and begins morphing into different shapes. The light suddenly fades and I'm left picturing nothing but darkness. I'm no longer on the beach, and there's nothing beside me. Thinking I did this completely wrong, I open my eyes, ready to whine to Mother, when something with velvet-like fur rubs against my ankle.

"I did it!" I lift the animal into my arms and snuggle him into my cheek. "He is so soft, I love him!"

Mother chuckles as she quietly approaches me and my familiar.

"You astound me every day, little one. You share Nan's features, you share her spirit, and now it seems, you also share her familiar." Her eyes are on me, but her mind is elsewhere.

"What do you mean?" I ask while petting the top of his head, right between his ears.

"Nan's familiar was a small rabbit named Beauty."

Beauty.

A name fit for the friend of a princess raised in a castle. I glance at the, definitely not small, rabbit in my arms. His gray fur shines under the sun and his white speckled feet rest on my arms. I look down into his blue eyes and feel more complete than I ever have in my life. He raises his nose to my mouth and his whiskers tickle my cheeks as he sniffs me.

"What's his name?" She whispers, reaching out to pet his fuzzy, little nose.

She told me this morning that we don't choose the names for our familiars, they already have them and we have to search within ourselves to realize what they are. I let him jump out of my arms onto the beach and watch as he makes his way over to Mead.

They sniff each other and then nuzzle their heads, immediately taking to one another. I focus on my rabbit and look into his eyes as he stands on his hind legs, now significantly taller than Mead. I can feel the connection between us, it feels like when he is away from me—even at such a small distance—there's a part of me that's missing. There's comfort in knowing he is near, and like a whisper through the wind, his name graces my thoughts.

"Frey, his name is Frey," I say confidently.

"A fitting name for the familiar of a Princess blessed by the Gods." My mother echoes my thoughts on Beauty. "You remind me so much of my grandmother. It warms my heart to see her in you. She would be so proud of you."

I step beside her and rest my head on her shoulder. "I wish she were here. Imagine if we were able to give her back her throne." I can feel her shaking her head in disagreement and wrapping her arm around my shoulders—in her safety and warmth.

"I don't think she would take it, little one. She was incredibly happy being settled down with Pa and teaching the village children. She felt safe and comfortable, but more importantly, this was the only place she really felt at home—after what happened to her family...her previous life."

"She wouldn't be alone though. We would go with her and be there." I imagine our family gathered around a huge hearth in a large castle suite. Our familiars chasing around each other, Nan and Pa snuggle on a settee, Mother and I challenging each other in a game of cards.

"Aye, but that isn't what she wanted. I think it would have been horribly traumatizing for her to return to the place her parents were killed, to work in her mother's office where she saw it happen. After years of the Regent tainting the castle, I doubt it would have been remotely welcoming to her."

I nod, understanding what she means. Her and I skip nearly all village events that take place in the market square after what happened to my father—not because we want to distance ourselves from our friends, but the fear that fun could turn to tragedy in less than a second clings to us like rain. I can't imagine being forced to be in that place every day for the rest of my days.

"I'm glad she chose to stay here with Pa. She deserved to be in such a peaceful place after everything. Another thing I have in common with her, but I'll make sure there's a different outcome."

My mother's arms tighten around my shoulders, her pride in my decision evident in the comfort she offers me.

"I agree, little one. She deserved the world, and Pa helped provide that while she created the life that she wanted here. She had a kind heart, one not meant for war or the adventures that lie ahead for us. Yet, she will always be a symbol to this Kingdom. One of hope, resilience, and wisdom."

Strong, slow clapping suddenly comes from behind us. Underneath my favorite maple tree is Pa, looking fondly at Frey now beside me.

"Woah Annie, great job sweetheart! You managed that just about as quick as yer mother did! Tessa was a bit slow on the uptake." He pretends to be in thought of past familiar meetings he's been witness to, his grin is a sly one, intent on lifting me up.

"What can I say, she gets the good powers handed down from me." Mother says with a shrug and an equally mischievous smile.

"Well, it would be odd if she didn't. Even your grandmother said your powers would surpass her own before you could even manage them. Your blood is a little more blessed than your ancestors it seems."

"Oh, get off it, old man. I'm no more powerful than any other Asvalda before me. I just have a bit more motivation than those before us to make sure my magic is as strong as it can be. Nothing more."

Mother begins turning toward our cabins as she speaks, no longer indulging our jokester grandsire. I notice him watching her carefully as she walks away, the gleam in his eyes turning into concern and wonder in an instant. He has had much to worry himself with in the last couple of decades, but when he looks at my mother, there is a different kind of concern there.

"The way you look at her—you teased about her powers and being more blessed than the others. Is there truth behind your words? Is that why worry glazes your eyes even now?" My words come out close to a whisper as I lean against the other side of the Maple's trunk. I cannot see his face as he replies, but in the way his exhale travels through the air, I can tell he has much to say. Things that he possibly kept bottled up for who knows how long.

"Oh, it's just a theory, Annie. But it's hard to deny how strong her magic is. I've only seen my wife and daughter's work, so it's hard to compare, but Nan swore that no one in her line had magic like yer mother. The power that radiates from her is so strong ya feel like you can touch it in the air." He pauses briefly, almost like he's in deep thought. "Has she ever told you the story about how Nan got her powers for the first time?"

"No, I never thought about asking either." I roll my eyes but cannot deny that I understand why such important information was kept from me. I'm grateful in a way. It left my childhood as carefree as it could be after losing my father in such a horrific battle.

"Aye, the story would've told you who Nan was immediately. She got her powers without even knowin' it, it happened so quickly. The moment she sensed the threat in the castle, Beauty appeared. Nan thought it was odd that a bunny was wanderin' in the thrall's tunnels but didn't realize it was her own familiar guidin' her." Pa takes a few steps forward and sits in front of the tree I'm leaning against.

I lower myself beside him and nod for him to continue. My mother may be in denial about her strength, but our family is aware of something deeper than she wants to admit, and there's nothing that will stop me from hearing the evidence. Finding out who we really are has me starving for information.

"Asvaldan magic has always appeared to the heirs in different ways. The more efficient way, according to yer family's library, has been when there is a strong surge of emotion—like fear. The day the King and Queen were murdered was a terrifying experience for Nan. She had watched her eighteenth birthday pass with no magic to be seen 'til that day, a fortnight later than she should've. Tessa was the same, her magic didn't appear 'til two months afterward and all she could do was light some candles." Looking down between his bent knees, he reaches and twists blades of grass together.

He doesn't continue his tale right away as he twirls the thin pieces through his fingertips either in deep thought, or maybe for the dramatics. Pa does love to tell a good story.

"And my mother? When—how did she get her magic?"

Pa smirks at the intense interest in my tone.

"Bree showed signs of magic when she was a young girl. We all saw the proof of it. Tessa met Bree's father on a trip and never saw him again, but that one time left her with a swollen belly. She was a single mother, with the help of myself and Nan of course, until she met another. The piece of shite had no love for Bree and you'll never convince me he ever loved Tessa either." The grass in Pa's hands snap with his anger toward the man.

"That's when the magic began. She protected herself without even knowin' what she could do. The good for nothin' bastard didn't know our family secret, thank the Gods, so we hid it as best we could. It was just little things for years–rain stopping when she wanted to play outside, becoming unfindable when her stepfather was looking for her, and somehow eatin' sweets off her plate when we definitely put vegetables on it. After a few years went by, we realized that her pet cat should have been getting on in age, but the little rascal lived years longer than any ordinary house cat should have. Bree needed her, so she lived for her."

How could any of that be possible? How can our entire lineage be granted their magic in adulthood yet she gained hers as a youngling? The tone Pa speaks in sews the truth for me, his voice has no trace of exaggeration, but instead, is filled with something rare for him–pure awe.

"What's different about my mother compared to all the others?" And could it be within myself as well? He mentioned that Nan and Tessa were both late gaining their powers, but I got mine the same day I became a woman.

"My guess is her father. We know nothin' about the man and he's the only outlier. Tessa was convinced that the Gods simply chose Bree as the heir to reclaim the throne, and in order to do that, they made her stronger than ever. More magic in her body than blood. Tessa lived by her theory, constantly left to go who knows where looking for who knows what. Her and Jaris were up to somethin' and I have a feeling it was to make sure things were ready for Bree."

"Is that where Tessa went after Nan died?"

He makes eye contact with me—the way his eyebrows furrow and jaw slackens, the undiluted joy in his eyes, I can tell he is nothing short of relieved. Someone is listening to him and understands exactly where his thoughts have been.

"My thoughts exactly, Annie. They never kept me in the loop with whatever they were doin', so I had no clue where to even begin looking for her. Jaris said he expected her to meet with him after Nan's funeral, but that was the last anyone saw of her." Worry drowns the joy in his irises, as it has for so long.

"Do you think Mother learned what they were up to? I know she plans to head for Frostheim to meet with Uncle Jaris, but that's as far as my knowledge goes."

"If she knew exactly what they were doin', then she wouldn't have lingerin' doubt in her mother like she does. There's a great chance Tessa was captured by the enemy–whether she's still alive today or not is impossible to know. Bree knows this is a possibility, even fears it. But she cannot stop the memory that plagues her...being abandoned by Tessa."

Mother has rarely voiced how she feels about Tessa in my presence, she does not wish to force any opinions on me when I have had no chance to feel otherwise. Yet, it's impossible not to notice her shoulders stiffen when Tessa is mentioned. It's the unfortunate consequence of our close relationship, she cannot hide her true feelings from me, no matter how hard she tries.

"My son will want to meet with Bree so that he can pass his mission with his sister on to her. Arm her with his knowledge and whatever it is they were been preparin' for, includin' the army he commands."

From some distance, my mother shouts for us to come to breakfast. She shamelessly adds a few threats of endearment since we're expected at the far beach for my party soon. As I turn toward our cabin, Pa's hand grips my wrist tightly and pulls me back to him.

"One last thing you should know–I suspect I won't have another chance to tell ya before ya leave." His voice is hushed and hurried, urgency possessing his words. "The night your father died confirmed my theory of yer mother. Her power is matched only by the Regent himself."

My heart races with my rising adrenaline at the mention of the solstice festival. His eyes bore into mine, making sure I cling to every word from his mouth. "The draugr were his creation–his dark magic. The moment your father fell to the ground, so did they."

"W–what? I don't remember that. I heard the swords—the fighting." My heart threatens to leap out of my chest.

"No Annie, you heard us cuttin' the heads from their necks as they were unmoving on the ground. You heard us sheath our weapons and search to make sure there were no more, kicking aside their weapons as we went."

"But—how? That doesn't make any sense. We would have seen that, she would know that she did that—" I desperately dig through the memory of my father's death for the truth, but I can see nothing but the blood spitting from his lips—my entire focus only on him.

"Just as she knew what she did as a child? No Annie, she was watching the love of her life take his last breaths and speak his final words. She focused on making sure he would make it to Valhalla and memorizing her last moment with him. The entire village saw what she did that night and suddenly—they knew. No one has ever spoken a word to her about it, at my request. She single handedly took down a small army of the undead with nothing but her grief. With one uncontrolled emotion, she combated the darkest magic this world has seen and she didn't even know she did it."

He loosens his grip around my wrist and straightens his back—standing tall. "There's more than just the passing down of a blessing from the Gods in my granddaughter. The blood of a God flows through her veins, I'm sure of it."

TWELVE
BREE

Walking through Skogby beside Pa would make anyone feel like royalty—everyone here loves and adores him. For decades, he's been the only blacksmith for both Skogby and Gledibyr, leaving many to rely on him.

I admire my grandfather's charisma as I walk arm in arm with him—one last time before we embark on the looming journey ahead. The way conversations flow when he's speaking with vendors. The details he knows about each person here. The way everyone seems to know and respect him. I'm proud to have such an honorable man as my grandfather.

As we approach the smithy, Annie takes his other arm and looks up at him with similar admiration in her gaze. "Pa, you would've made a wonderful king. Everyone loves you!"

"Oh Annie, that wouldn't have been the life for me. Although, I would have done my best if Nan wanted to go back. I wouldn't be the man you see today without her anyway." He squeezes her hand and limps over to the fireplace, grabbing a stoker and a box of matches.

"Annie, help Pa get things cleaned up a little bit down here please, I'll be upstairs preparing our beds." I wait for her nod before turning toward the stairs.

As I head up the stairs to the apartment, I'm hit with a wave of nostalgia and guilt. The last time I stayed overnight here was for a romantic "getaway" with Des. We spent the day shopping, got properly sloshed at the pub, and spent the rest of the night together in bed. Looking around the bedroom makes my heart suddenly feel empty. I long for my other half to walk through the door and make me laugh again, to remind me of the kind of love that completely takes over your soul, wrapping it in a safe, loving embrace.

His booming laugh filled the room with happiness and warmth. I drag my fingers across the cool bricks of the fireplace, reminiscing about another time we stayed here and sat by the fire to wait out a sudden storm that hit while I was selling some new maps I designed. He wrapped a fur blanket around my shoulders and came up with about five different ways to make me laugh so hard I peed myself and had to take a hot bath.

"What are you laughing at?" A soft voice asks.

"I just remembered a time when your father and I stayed the night here . He made me laugh so hard I peed on that chair." When I turn to face my daughter she offers me a sad smile, walking over to take my hand in her own.

"He could make anyone laugh, your father. His humor is something I miss immensely. Lucky for me, he seems to have passed that gift on to his daughter." A gleam shines in Annie's eyes at my words and she stands a little taller than before. "Well, enough of that. Let's get the place tidied up so we can make some food and get a good night's sleep." I pick my bag up where I left it by the stairs and place it on the chair to get it out of the way.

"Glad you are using that chair. I don't want my things to smell of stale piss," she snickers.

"Annalysa Ragna! I will have you know that I washed this chair very well, your father even helped, empathetic to the fact it was his fault in the first place." I am trying, and failing, to keep the laughter out of my voice and stop my smile in its tracks. The last thing my daughter needs to know is that her attitude amuses me, something she inherited from Destrin.

"I've seen what that man considered to be 'clean'. I'm not impressed."

Alas, the laughter is stronger than I, and Annie's face glows with triumph.

"You speak nothing short of the truth, my dear."

"Have you sent word to Jaris about your plan?" Pa asks with his mouth half full of the turkey he just finished cooking.

"Last word I sent informed him of our tentative departure. He knows to expect us within one moon cycle from Annie's birthday. Taking time for any possible unforeseen circumstances that may arise into account."

Annie places her fork on the table slowly, clearing her throat and looking at me for what I assume is comfort. "I actually wanted to speak with you about what to expect on the journey, besides the obvious being the Regent."

Pa glances at me in surprise, figuring Annie should already know this information. I return his look with a glare, sometimes it astounds me that he doesn't expect me to be prepared, "I think one thing we can expect to encounter is draugr. After the festival, I'm sure they are a favorite of his. There are plenty of lesser fae that hide in forests we need to watch out for as well." Unease is written across her face as she chews her breakfast slowly. Pa just looks down at his hands with a certain smugness in his grin, knowing he taught us how to fight and counter many different creatures of the dark.

"As we embark on this journey you need to remember three very important things. First, you need to trust your instincts—we have magic within us and it guides us. Our instincts are fueled by our magic and thus, will never lie. Second, evil likes to hide in the shadows amongst the good—it's important that you shouldn't give your trust freely. Lastly, we will no doubt face incredible challenges and it is so, so important that you always make the best decision for the entire Kingdom, not just yourself. Do you understand?"

I see a future Queen in my daughter, and it's not for the first time. Her lips form a tight line and she gives me a curt nod, ready to face the coming danger and do what she must in order to achieve our goal.

Pa grabs her hand and squeezes it with pride. "Ah, there she is. My girl." I can't help but wonder if my grandfather's words are because he sees the shift in Annie that occurred, or because he sees the resemblance to Nan while he looks at her. I can't help but see both as power and confidence emanates from her.

She will be our Queen—she will be our salvation.

THIRTEEN

ANNIE

The morning greets us with crisp air and a bright sky as we approach the stables where Pa has paid for our horses. After securing my packs, I attempt to toss myself onto the saddle for the third time until I finally turn and see my family watching me, barely containing their laughter. I shoot them a stern glare, only for it to break my mother's inner battle and make her face light up. That smile of hers is so rare that it catches me off guard, making my third attempt just as unsuccessful as the previous two.

"Oh come on, Annie, I know I taught you better than that. Just get up on the horse! How do you expect to save the world when you can't even ride?" Pa's words are dripping with sarcasm and now his mask is broken as well. They both chuckle as they come closer to show me what I was doing wrong.

"You aren't bending at the knee enough. You need to use momentum rather than trying to just pull yourself up. You could hurt yourself and your horse. Watch your mother."

She walks up to her own horse and mounts so quickly and gracefully that it looks as if an invisible force simply plucked her from the ground and placed her gently on the horse's back. She shoots me a challenging grin, raising an eyebrow as if to tell me to do better. There's no way her mount was *that* perfect, she used magic and is now expecting me to attempt the same with my budding powers.

Not one to stand down, I grab the pommel of the saddle and close my eyes. I imagine the ball of light growing bigger and bigger until I can feel it flowing through my veins like it did when I met Frey—making me as light as a feather.

"Annie, that was cheating, but it was an impressive use of your magic."

Opening my eyes, I realize I made it onto my horse and did it solely with my powers. Mother smiles at me with such pride that I can't help but sit a bit straighter.

"It's not cheating if it works, I believe that is something you also taught me, Pa." At that, my mother erupts with laughter and Pa rubs his calloused hand over his balding head in defeat.

"You got me there, kiddo. Be safe you two, and do Nan justice when you get to that sniveling coward of a man. The next time I see you girls there better be crowns on your heads and a regal meal with all of that fancy ale they must have in the castle waiting for me."

Mother smiles and squeezes his hand in a final goodbye. "You deserve nothing less for all you've done for our family. We love you, and be safe as well."

My horse trots forward and a nervous chill dances over my skin. I'm leaving home for the first time in my life. I turn in my saddle to get one last look at Pa—only the Gods know when we will see each other again. I'm more than excited for adventure and the unknown, but I summon Frey for added comfort anyway.

We begin our journey riding next to each other down the village path toward the trail that will lead us out of Skogby and into the forest that protects its borders. The weight of my father's golden arm ring suddenly feels heavy on my wrist, like it's aware of the destined quest we have begun.

It's almost like it knows what is to come, and it's reminding me that my father will be here with us every single step of the way. Thinking of him, I sense his presence among us, seeing us safely off into the world. It's a small brush of a breeze through my hair, but I know he is here, walking beside Frey and his girls.

We've been riding through the forest for only a few hours and my backside is already in protest. Mother says we won't stop until the sun is preparing to set. Only then will we eat and head directly to bed for an early start tomorrow. According to one of her intricate maps she designed, it should take us a little more than two days of riding until we arrive at the inn we'll be staying at in Huginnstead. I have the map perched between my legs, on my horse's neck, so I can study it as we ride, hoping it's somehow wrong and I can get off this creature sooner. Although it's highly unlikely, she's an expert for a reason.

The sun shines in a thousand rays through the tree cover above, and we see all kinds of wildlife as we ride along the dirt road. Deer watch us through the foliage closer to the path and birds sing to each other as they fly overhead. Everything is so calm here, and I think this is an excellent way to begin our mission—although I shouldn't fool myself into thinking it will be like this the entire way. Thinking back to our conversation at dinner last night, I decide I want to hear another story about our Kingdom.

Out of the corner of my eye, I notice my mother is staring very intently into the trees, almost as if she's looking for something.

"What is it?" I ask, worry lacing my words—hoping we are not about to face an obstacle so soon.

"I'm not sure. I just have a feeling that something is close. I can't tell if it's malicious or not. I just feel...something." She shakes her head and looks forward again, not disregarding her feelings but setting it aside in her head to re-evaluate as we go. She notices me watching her and gives a tight smile. "Nothing to worry about, Annie. Just be aware and try to use this as an opportunity to hone your own magic. It can help you sense these things as well. This is a useful power to wield because almost nothing can outsmart your instincts."

"I'm not worried. I trust you." I glance forward down the path we are following and try to project my power away from myself, sensing the nature and wildlife around us. A strange warmth tingles my skin. A soft hum of life flows through the trees and wildflowers. The bird songs are suddenly louder and more pronounced, fluttering wings sound as if they soar past my ears. I become one with the life around me and search for anything that may seem out of place.

There are two small beings not far from us, their aura different from all of the others in the forest, but I don't sense anything wrong about them. If anything, they feel like they are supposed to be there, like I *need* them to be.

I relay my findings to Mother, brows furrowing as she listens closely. By the end of my explanation her jaw is tight.

"Annie...that is absolutely incredible. You're already able to wield your magic at an extraordinary level." She looks forward in thought, contemplating what the beings are. Scanning the trees, I don't see any odd movement or watchful eyes, only Frey in my peripheral, following loyally. Hopefully my instincts are accurate.

After a bit of deeper thought, I remember I originally was going to ask for a story before we got distracted. "Mother, can you tell me a story from our people to pass the time?"

After a grimace and a questioning expression she reluctantly agrees. "I suppose I can—keep in mind that my story telling is nothing like Pa's, but I'll try my best. Do you want to hear the tale behind the serpent your father's arm ring represents?"

My ears perk with interest and I give her all of my attention, nodding for her to continue.

"That's the World Serpent, Jörmungandr. He's a son of the Trickster God, Loki. He has two infamous siblings, the giant wolf known as Fenrir and the Goddess of the dead, Hel. It's said the trio was brought before the ruler of Gods, Odin."

"You see, there's a prophecy where the downfall of Odin and the other Gods is caused by these siblings. This prophecy is now known as Ragnarök, and it casts a deep rooted fear into the heart of Odin, causing him to punish Loki's children in unimaginable ways. Fenrir was cast in inescapable chains made by dwarves. Hel was sent to Niflheim—the realm of the dead. And Jörmungandr was thrown into the sea to drown. But rather than succumbing to this fate, he grew to an unimaginable size—so large that he's able to wrap his body around our world and grasp his tail in his mouth, creating the Ouroboros. The army wears these on their wrists to show their similarity with Jörmungandr in a way. They too, surround our world—in protection rather than threat"

I touch the head of the serpent that makes up my arm ring and notice how intricate the details that create the scales are and the piercing, angry eyes.

"The World Serpent loathes not only Odin for what he has done to him, but also the God of thunder, Thor. A giant once made a mockery of both the serpent and the god, making quick work of disappearing soon after creating conflict, leaving the two to aim their hatred at each other rather than the true culprit, thus beginning their infinite feud." She takes a dramatic pause, surveying the trees around us once more.

"Thor has since tried luring Jörmungandr out from the seas in order to kill him, but has been thwarted each time. It is said that Jörmungandr lays in wait until his siblings are ready to enact their revenge on the Gods who did this to them. When certain prophetic signs occur; Fenrir will break free of his chains. Hel will march her army of the dead to Midgard, and Jörmungandr will join his siblings, signaling the apocalyptic battle, Ragnarök. Thor will ultimately achieve his goal in killing the Midgard Serpent at the cost of his own life. After only nine steps he will fall to the ground, lifeless. Both enemies will be defeated and neither will be champion. This is the prophecy that made Odin banish the children of Loki in the first place."

"It almost sounds like the entire thing could have been avoided if Odin hadn't ostracized Loki's children like that." I meant this as a statement but it comes across more like a question instead. The corner of her mouth pulls up, content with my conclusion of the tale.

"I agree, little one. Unfortunately, we cannot always see the outcome of our decisions, which is why we must always think before we act. Odin believed he was doing exactly what he needed to do in order to protect all of the life that he created. If these visions of Ragnarök prove to be true, then we will all have to deal with the consequences of his actions. Until then..." She pauses, "Well if and when Ragnarök happens, I just hope we are somehow spared. Although, it is meant to be the end of humanity."

Originally, when I wanted to hear a story I expected to feel at least slightly better afterward, maybe even excited. I surely hadn't expected I would be contemplating everything so differently in the world.

Odin is known for his wisdom and strength as a leader. Surely he would be confident in his foresight. Surely he would be able to choose the correct path to ensure the survival of mankind, his proudest creation.

With as many stories of our Gods we share with each other, I have never quite taken Ragnarök as seriously as I am at this moment. I had heard most of the stories when I was a young girl—maybe my inadvertent innocence protected me from the lessons that can be learned from them.

I will never be able suppress my laughter when I think about the almighty god of thunder teaming up with the god of trickery to dress up as ladies so they could trick a couple of giants into returning his hammer, Mjölnir. That is the story she should've told as we travel, we could use a few laughs.

After a few more hours of riding and storytelling, I'm absolutely certain those two strange auras have been following us the entire way. I know my mother is aware of their presence as well. It's odd they don't give her the same comfort they give me. When I close my eyes and push my magic away from myself, I can see their energy more clearly. They give off a strong plum colored light and have the shine of a fire sprite. They soar between the branches in a swirling pattern like they're dancing through the forest beside us, so close that I should easily be able to see them when I open my eyes, but there's nothing. Only the same trees with the same animals scurrying past and no special aura radiating from them at all.

Except something *is* different.

The sunlight that was shining through the branches above us fades to darkness in seconds, despite it still being the middle of the day. The colorful and comforting life that has surrounded us the entire day is now silent, the only sound in the forest coming from the dried leaves as they are blown along the ground by a chilled breeze—whistling as it forces past us. The horses are clearly unhappy with the sudden drop in temperature, and begin to walk faster—as if they know exactly what is causing the sudden change in weather.

"Stay alert, Annie. Whatever is happening now is unnatural," mother warns.

The auras I've been tracking thus far drift away from us. Their dance becomes a flurry of distress as they attempt to come closer but are blocked by something. A new aura emerges, surrounding us in shadows and a tunnel made from the dead leaves trails the forest floor. The trees disappear behind the forceful winds while the shadows weave through the twister—pungent with the stench of death and despair. My hair twists in fury around my face and neck, and my horse whinnies in terror.

All at once, everything stops.

There is no breeze, there are no leaves. No light, no fright, just a sense of unease. The forest has turned so black that I can't see my hand in front of my face. I attempt to call for Mother but nothing leaves my lips—my heart begins to race in anxious terror. The only thing I can feel is my horse beneath me, although it lacks any warmth from its hide or the steady rise and fall of its breathing. There is absolutely nothing in this stagnant darkness besides my consciousness and I have never felt more trapped.

Just as I am about to turn myself over to panic, a warmth slowly creeps back. Two purple orbs dance around us once again, a glittery shine following their form. The terror tucks its tail as the two auras waltz about, embracing me with the feeling of hope, excitement, and protection. As they close in, I hear an enthusiastic whisper speak directly into my thoughts:

"She's here! She's found!
She conquers the ground!

She watches close,
To where we are bound.
The hiding is done,
So here comes the fun!
Be careful now...
The Regent has come."

The flutter of wings beat against my hair and tiny claws dig into my shoulder. Something brushes against my ear and what feels like the beak of a bird pushes against my cheek, trying to make sure it has my full attention as it perches on my shoulder. A deeper whisper suddenly recites:

"The Blessed have returned,
Their grief marks their souls.
Love pushes forth,
New dawn from the old.
The soldier is gone,
Yet two more emerge.
One from birth,
The other with surge.
A battle they yearn,
Where the demons will flock,
Everything ends in Ragnarök*."*

FOURTEEN
BREE

I'm off my horse before she can hit the ground.

"Annie!" I yell as I catch her, protecting her head from hitting a protruding root.

As soon as the darkness dissipated, Annie gasped and came into view, sliding off her horse looking dazed. As I look at her now, her lips move in an indiscernible manner while her eyes move rapidly behind closed lids.

I frantically look around the trees surrounding us, searching for whatever caused the darkness and inevitably my daughter's fainting spell. The natural sounds of the forest have returned as well as the warmer temperature. The tension weighing in the air has calmed—all that is left is for Annie to wake. She said earlier that the auras she sensed were protecting her, I can only assume they're the reason for the shadow creature's disappearance.

There were whispers with the voices of men before reality returned and I only heard one thing very clearly...

Ragnarök.

The end of us all and the triumph of no one.

There's a loud caw from a raven. It emerges from the forest and lands on my daughter's shoulder as another perches on mine. As soon as they land I notice that her breathing begins to slow, her eyes are going still, but her lips rest in a break from her silent whispers.

The raven on her begins poking around softly with its black beak as if trying to help wake her. As I make eye contact with the other raven, I notice a gleam in its eye as it nods at me—almost to tell me that everything will be okay. These must be the protectors she sensed in the shadows. Something about them feels oddly familiar, like I know them. I couldn't discern what I felt when I sensed them before, but now there's no question. I feel as though I am stuck in a trance as the raven looks deeply into my eyes, as I do theirs. They can sense it too, whatever this familiarity is, and although their faces cannot give way to emotion, it's evident to me that they're just as struck by this as I am.

Annie shuffles in my arms and moans as if waking from a fitful sleep. She begins lifting her head, her hand moving to shield her eyes from the sunlight. The moment she realizes there's a bird standing on her, her shoulders tense and she freezes. Rather than seeming afraid or confused, she reaches a hand out to the raven that made its way to her chest and slowly turns her head to face the other mischievous creature.

"Was...were those whispers from you two?" Annie whispers.

The pair caws in response and spread their wings in unison, preparing to take off back into the sky or wherever they choose to linger. The first raven takes off with the second following close behind, swirling through the air in a choreographed manner until they are hidden in the foliage once more.

"They will stay nearby, no doubt. I'm assuming their auras were the ones you have felt this whole time?" I implore.

"Y-yes. They whispered to me in the darkness...a warning, I think." Her voice wavers as she rises from the dirt and brushes the palms of her hands on her pants. "They spoke in rhymes, as if they were reciting a poem. They said the Regent has come and they spoke of Ragnarök..."

Her words run through my thoughts, trying to make sense of what specifically they could be warning us about. The Regent is not in these woods and we are already aware that he is a threat to everything we aim for–the reason for everything we have lost thus far.

The shadows...those were born of magic. Does the Regent have traps set amongst the trails surrounding the last known area of the Lost Princess?

"I think... I think they mentioned father. One said, *'The soldier is gone, yet two more emerge. One from birth, and the other with surge'*. That has to be our family. Father died, he began training me as soon as I could walk, and trained you to fight as well." Her voice becomes airy as her words pick up speed in her realizations.

He trained me himself and I did nothing.
I could have helped him.
I could have protected him.
He should be here.

I push my poisonous thoughts from the forefront of my mind as memories of sweat soaked tunics, swollen eyes and blistered hands flood my sight, bringing me back to the days of harsh training to assure I could defend myself and be an asset in battle. I knew I needed to learn as much as I possibly could and become a soldier in my own right. The ravens were surely speaking of our family and it sounds as if they could have been sharing a prophecy of their own.

I help Annie onto her horse and mount my own. Out of the corner of my eye I see her glancing in my direction repeatedly, most likely waiting for a response to her theory.

The truth is, I'm not sure what to say. These ravens will most likely make another appearance and all we can do is wait and see what happens. Why mention our fallen soldier, Destrin? Does he play some part in all of this, besides his death acting as a catalyst to push our family to take back the throne appointed to us by the Gods? He gave his life for us, he owes the Gods, Norns, whoever the Hel, nothing more. If his purpose was solely to bring the Asvalda's to action then I will curse the Gods myself when I arrive in Valhalla.

"They know something, Mother. They're on our side, they seemed overjoyed that we have come out of hiding—it makes me wonder if the rest of the kingdom will feel the same."

I nudge my horse in the side to start moving once I am assured Annie is safely in her saddle before finally acknowledging her.

"The people of this kingdom adored Nan's parents during their reign. Nan was their beloved princess and there were whispers of outrage when the Regent executed her publicly."

She flinches at my words, however harsh they may sound, now is not the time for pleasantries.

"Along with their anger came hope when they realized her power had not transferred to him when she was killed, for it meant there was still at least one living heir to save them from the usurper. So, yes Annie. They will be overjoyed when we rid the world of his filth and treachery and continue the legacy of our family."

Two days later, we exit the forest walls and arrive in Huginnstead without further incidents. It is a beautiful, bustling town that is easily twice the size of Skogby. The dirt path from the forest slowly transitions to gravel as we get closer to civilization, the crunch beneath the steeds' hooves is like a breath of fresh air as it means we are near a warm bed, a warm bath, and warm food.

As we approach, I spot the ravens in the sky, passing overhead and soaring straight above the taller buildings in town and out of sight. I've only visited this town once while traveling the kingdom in order to accurately chart my maps, and it's just as welcoming as I remember. If my memory serves correctly, there is a very well kept Inn towards the center of town that is surrounded by pubs, shops, and a delightful book shop.

Annie rides slightly ahead of me, clearly lost in her thoughts as we draw nearer to town. One of her hands grips the reins to her horse tightly while she has the other placed on her upper abdomen, right in the middle.

"What plagues your thoughts, little one? We'll soon have every comfort, yet you seem distracted."

"The ravens follow us still," She practically whispers in response. I have to lean forward and try to catch up to her in order to hear her next words, "They are a great comfort and yet their presence confuses me." She turns her body enough to face me, her hand still just below her chest. "I have this ball of nerves that sits right here. When it gets bad, it rises up my chest and into my throat. I cannot stop the tears that flow freely or the panic that grips my heart. Every foul emotion floods out of me until I feel empty and can only lay down while thinking to myself, 'What the Hel just happened'?"

My heart breaks for my daughter and I understand exactly what she's describing. It's an unfortunate quality of the Ragna Clan—to inherit constant fear for our lives every single day. It has only gotten worse since the loss of Nan and the disappearance of Tessa, but nothing will compare to the death of Destrin and it shows in both myself, and Annie.

"That is not what takes over my thoughts, that is just life. When these two ravens are near, and I see them flying over us like just a moment ago, the ball in my chest feels like it is so close to disintegrating. Like it's *so* close to not being a part of me anymore. They're here as a comfort and protection, I know it in my heart," She sits forward once again and looks back up at the sky where the ravens flew by just moments ago.

"When you fainted, I felt some kind of connection to them. They could feel it too, it was so strong that all three of us seemingly forgot what had just occurred, and could only stare into each other's eyes. They made me feel like everything would be okay." I glance to the sky, wondering if I'll catch them soaring past like she has.

"I'll ignore that you just admitted you forgot about me for some birds you just met. Continue, what did you feel?" She asks, her tone dripping with sarcasm.

"'Forgot' was the wrong choice of word, we were merely distracted. You would be too if you were convinced that you personally knew two ravens that you have never seen or sensed before." I throw her my best 'disgruntled mother' expression before turning my nose up at her and taking the lead.

I guide us through the busy streets to a public stable in between the inn and the most well-known pub in Huginnstead, The Elk's Head. Annie hops off of her horse with magical ease and I watch her proudly as she manifests her new magic so flawlessly. Just a few days ago she was too nervous to try to get on her horse using her magic and now, she manipulates it like she has been honing it for years. I wish Nan and Des were here to see her, I can't imagine how phenomenally she'd be able to wield her magic already if she had a proper teacher like Nan.

"Mother, I love you, but please stop looking at me like that and get off your horse. I am *famished*."

I can't help but chuckle, a direct imitation of her father. I do as she says and gather our things so we can head inside and get a room.

The Inn is filled with many tables, all taken by customers eating their dinner and delving into their drinks that will surely lead them over to The Elk's Head later tonight.

The inside of the building is much larger than most Inn's across the kingdom, excluding the large cities, and is clearly well cared for. Multiple waitresses tend to the twenty or so tables that fill the dining room, there are two large fireplaces on either side of the room with extravagant fires. One of the fireplaces is accompanied by multiple plump sitting chairs surrounding it. There's a grand bar off to the right where both men and women rest on wooden stools and laugh with the barmaid. The place is cozy, happy, and is a great first stop on our journey. A second barmaid comes toward us with a smile and asks politely if we need two rooms.

"One room please, with two beds. Can we dine here tonight as well?" I ask hopefully, knowing Annie wants to skip all of the small talk and get right to her food.

"We actually just finished serving the last of dinner, but The Elk's Head has the best pub food in all of Asvalda and they serve all night. Tell ole' Hank that Rita sent you over and he will give you a much fairer price than most." She hands us the key to our room and squeezes my shoulder with a warm smile. I hand the key to Annie and ask her to bring our things up to the room while I get a head start on ordering our food next door.

If I thought that the Inn was cozy, it's nothing compared to The Elk's Head. Plush couches surround a circular fireplace in the middle of the room where people lounge comfortably while laughing and drinking their hearts away. Booths line the side wall with curtains pulled to the side so that customers can close them for more private conversations. The mahogany bar takes up the entire back wall of the pub, the stools designed to look like they came directly from the forest with antlers for the legs and a mushroom top for the seat.

The wall behind the bar is made of matching mahogany and has a mounted elk head that has to be the largest I've ever seen. He watches over the establishment and its patrons—his pointed antlers almost touch the ceiling and his black leathery nose looks to be the size of my entire face. Despite his size, the elk looks incredibly inviting—and soft. There are three women working behind the bar, pouring ale and handing out food. An older man leans against the counter from their side and speaks with one of the customers, making each other laugh.

I make my way over to him with a smile. He becomes aware of my gaze and says goodbye to a customer, making his way over to an empty spot for me to speak with him.

"Did Rita send you this way?" His voice is deep with a hint of a smooth foreign accent rolling his R's.

"She did, how did you know?"

"Every night a few people wander in for their first time looking slightly lost and in awe of ole' Hank here." He points to the mounted elk. "He attracts quite a few fans. The food here helps too, we have a bit of a reputation and Rita sends her hungry guests our way as much as she can." He finishes off with a smile and begins to fill a pint of ale.

"The elk's name is Hank? I was under the impression that was you." He hands me the ale and I take a hearty sip.

"We're both Hank! This fella here has been on the wall for over a hundred years, give or take. My great-great-great grandpappy killed it and he swears he had to fight off giants to claim it himself. 'Splains why Hank here is so large anyway. He was so proud that he named it after himself, and then named his son Hank too. Ever since, every first born son has been named Hank in honor of him and this beautiful creature above my bar." Hank pats the side of the elk's neck proudly and turns his head to yell something to one of the women working regarding some bread.

Annie walks up to us and takes the empty seat beside me, staring at the elk in awe. Human Hank and I share a knowing grin while she looks upon the giant elk until she finally asks if I ordered any food yet.

"How do a couple of juicy chicken legs with some chopped oil fried potatoes sound? It's our best seller besides the ale for a reason." He says, pulling a pipe and tobacco from his pocket.

"That sounds delicious, and can I have an ale as well?" Annie can't hide the pure excitement for the upcoming meal in her voice, making Hank chuckle.

A moment after he leaves, one of the barmaids comes over with a small basket of bread and a thick red oil in a porcelain bowl. She sees our look of confusion and explains that we should try dipping the bread into the oil and taking a bite of it that way. We both rip off small pieces of bread and take a cautious bite after dipping it. Annie's eyes go wide and she immediately goes for another bite. The woman says the oil is a mix of tomatoes, garlic and a hint of spicy pepper—it's simply delectable.

"If we find new food like this all over the continent then I will be a *very* happy princess." She practically moans with her mouth stuffed with bread and oil. The rest of our food arrives quickly and my daughter eats like she'll never see food again.

"Careful with your words, Annie. Just because we whisper to each other doesn't mean that others cannot hear." I try to catch her eyes to imbue the severity of my words. "Nan whispered nothing, and yet the Regent still managed to find her. His man with dark magic found your father and I in Skogby. We can never be too careful, little one. Our journey is much too fragile at the moment to reveal ourselves to the world."

Darkness floods her face as she realizes her mistake. "You're right, I'll be more careful. In my defense, this food is to die for. I can't believe you've kept me away from this town my whole life, I could have been eating like a queen this whole time!" She dives back into her meal, reminding me once again of her late father, and I begin to eat as well.

Everything really is delicious, and with Hank staring across the bar overhead, I can't help but hope that we can continue with this comfort for as long as we possibly can.

FIFTEEN
BREE

Darkness consumes the corridor. Thin beams of moonlight shine through narrow windows that line the dreary brick wall. A velvet red carpet lies on the cold stone floor, urging me to follow its lead. Mead trots ahead of me, frequently looking behind him to ensure I'm still following closely. My senses are dull and my head is filled with fog. The only sounds in the vicinity are our soft footsteps and the flickering flame that lights a sconce down the hall.

Far...so far away.

The flame is...

I try to quicken my pace toward the light, following my familiar as quickly as I possibly can. He's walking too fast and it's impossible to make my legs move any faster. I feel as though I'm trying to run while chest deep in water, something is pushing against me, slowing me down.

Mead suddenly stops and turns to face me—sitting down directly in the middle of the corridor, in front of the lit sconce.

I made it...the light is right here.

Why did I need to get here?

Mead meows and when I look down at him, he dissipates into dark smoke that's escaping a wick freshly put out.

Heavy footsteps sound behind me, solid boots against wet stone. I try turning my body to face the possible threat, but an invisible force stops me from doing so. I can move nothing but my head and it will not reach far enough to see who approaches.

What—who is that?

A soft, deep hum fills my ears and dances through my mind. It twirls and fills my empty, broken heart. This symphony is everything. It envelops me in a warm embrace and helps me join in its performance. I never want it to leave; I never want to stop hearing this beautiful voice that tells me I'm loved and strong and that everything will be okay.

Because it won't be okay.

He's gone.

This isn't real.

"I am as real as the fear in your heart, my beautiful, warrior wife."

Rough, calloused hands touch my bare shoulders in a gentle caress. Thick, coarse hair grazes from his cheek to mine as he hums into my ear and places a kiss on my temple.

"I am as real as the mountains, the sea, and the sun." He continues, his hands sliding down my arms until they find their familiar hold on my hips. His mouth hovers only an inch away from mine. I want to turn and kiss him, but I am stopped once more.

"You're gone..." I whisper, tears silently racing down my cheek.

"I have never been gone, my love. I have always been right here." He places one hand above my heart while the other stays on my hip. Warmth spreads through my chest at his touch and the tears fall faster as a broken sob racks through me.

"I have never left your side. I've been witness to you raising our daughter. I sit beside you when you visit me by the sea, and I will be right by your side forevermore." He shifts his body so he is finally in front of me, allowing me to finally see his face after so many years. He looks exactly as he did before he died, yet somehow more handsome than I remember.

Both of his hands find either side of my face as he brings his forehead down to meet mine. He closes his eyes but I cannot. If I close them, he will disappear again. I haven't been able to gaze upon my other half in far too long to not bask in every single second that he stands before me.

"You should be here with us, I failed you. I-"

He places a finger across my lips, cutting me off.

"You have never come close to failing me for as long as we've known each other. I gave everything I could to protect you and Annie and that is all I ever wanted to be able to do." He places stray hair behind my ear and uses his thumb to wipe away another fallen tear. A large sigh escapes him as he lifts his head, pressing his lips against my forehead. "Bree, nothing could have been different about that night. Whether you fought or not, you still would've had to leave with Annie and I still would have stopped the draugr."

His words are laced with logic and yet, I still can't accept them. I know that leaving Annie alone in the world with just Pa would have been significantly worse for her. Growing up with the fate that has been left to us is enough on its own. If I had died alongside Destrin then I would have caused Annie even more trauma and heartbreak. Would she have been ready to move against the Regent after all of these years as we do now?

Mead reappears, slipping between our legs and wrapping his tail around Des' shin. We glance down at him, and he meets our gazes with a quiet meow accompanied with a look that tells us our reunion is coming to an end. Realizing I need to say goodbye to my love again *makes my heart race and chest tighten. Noticing the panic, Destrin wraps his arms tightly around me and kisses the top of my head.*

"Know this, wife. You will never be alone in this war, and that is what is coming. He knows you have left the protection of Gledibyr and has already begun his hunt for you. You will have allies at every corner, but you will also discover how horrific this world has become under his

reign." He begins to back away from me, into the dark corridor with only the moonlight.

"Des, wait!"

"I will not kiss you tonight, my love. When I kiss you again it will be when we are reunited in the afterlife, and the wait will be well worth it." He continues to back away with a sad countenance, only a sliver of remaining moonlight offering me one last glance of him, of the confidence and pride he has in me. He places his hand on his chest, directly over his heart. In his smooth baritone voice he whispers once more...

"Always right here, my love."

SIXTEEN
ANNIE

By the time I wake, my mother is already dressed and ready for the day ahead. I suppose I should at least attempt to appreciate early mornings now, there are very few late morning lounging opportunities when you're traveling by horse across a kingdom.

"Come along, Annie. We need to send word to Uncle Jaris that we are on our journey to him and to search for us if we don't arrive." She speaks as she begins packing my sack with my discarded day clothes from the previous day.

"That's not depressing to think about at all." I reply sarcastically. If there's any way to start off the day it definitely shouldn't be thinking about our impending disappearance or death.

"Everything is depressing Annie, that's why we're doing this. Get moving, I left a basin of water for you to wash up before we go if you'd like."

I dramatically stretch my way out of bed and over to the water she spoke of. With no privacy or time to fully bathe, I simply splash water on my face to wake myself up and change into my clothes for the day that my mother so graciously left out for me when she was re-packing my things.

When we make it outside the Inn, Mother sets off at a brisk pace toward a small shop across the town that houses a variety of messenger birds. When I ask why there are so many different types for the same task, the elderly caretaker responds with, "Well ya don't expect this tiny little thing to survive all the way from here to Frostheim, do ya? Nah lass, that's a job for one of the doves. Use that brain o' yers."

Before I can respond, my mother snickers and shoves me out the front door and sends me on the task to grab us some breakfast, surely to keep me from ruining our opportunity to send word to Uncle Jaris by proving to the disrespectful man why I shouldn't use this brain of mine to form an elaborate insult too intelligent for his shriveled head.

It doesn't take long to discover the scent of fresh bread and follow it instinctually. Only a few buildings down sits an adorable bakery with what seems to be hundreds of different pastries and breads. While off to the side is a wall full of flavored jams and local honey to garnish the treats.

"It will take an army for her to get me to leave this place..." I say to myself as I try to decide what I should start my four course breakfast off with.

"Well then it's a good thing we are on our way to get an army, isn't it?" So focused on all of the baked goods, I didn't even hear my mother approach. "Pick a few things and let's move along, it will take us another two days to reach Lakewood and I doubt you want to have to camp two nights in a row."

I absolutely do not.

I pick up as much as I can fit into my arms and bring the pile of pastries over to pay and have it wrapped. Wisely, my mother has no smart remarks about my armfuls of food. She knows some of it is for her and she also knows that one of my greatest weaknesses is the bottomless pit known as my stomach. A trait I am so often told was graciously gifted to me by my father, as well as Pa.

Our walk back to the stables is thankfully at a reasonable pace so that we can walk and talk about our next steps. The goal is to head to Lakewood next, a town that is named for exactly what it is, a lake surrounded by woods.

It's primarily stocked with travel supplies, prepared rations, and log cabins used by all of the hunters that travel there annually to try to find the legendary monster who resides in the snow. It is famous in the surrounding towns and strikes fear into the hearts of many, so there is a competition every year with a grand reward for anyone who is able to capture or kill the creature–which has never been done. A bit barbaric if you ask me. I don't understand why it cannot be allowed to live its life, if it is even real to begin with.

The supplies in Lakewood are catered specifically for people who are attempting to cross into the snowy barren land, The Frostreik, that leads to Frostfjord and Frostheim—two towns facing each other with the Great Lake separating them. The journey through The Frostreik is going to be dreadful–neither of us have any wish to dredge through snow for days on end.

Not only do we plan on having to travel through the Frostreik, but we'll also be skipping the paths altogether and opting for a more scenic and deadly route that will hopefully bring us right to Frostheim so that we can bypass Frostfjord altogether. Mother says if we continue on those paths, it would be just as dangerous as the pathless snowy mountains because it would bring us dangerously close to the outskirts of Skalborg, where the Jarl there would recognize my mother in seconds. So perilous mountains it is, and hopefully Jaris finds us before we freeze to death.

"Annie, stop being dramatic and think about this logically." Mother drawls when I tell her my thoughts. "If we can make it up the mountains without having to go entirely around the Great Lake and close enough to Skalborg where the Jarl's men will surely be stationed, just to make it to the paths up the mountain to Frostheim itself, then we can save ourselves from inevitable torture and misery if we're caught. If we fail and perish trying to climb the sides of the mountains then I can promise you, it is a far more merciful death than what would be brought upon us if that man got ahold of us—even before handing us over to the Regent."

The tone in her voice silences me. She has always had a high tolerance for my shenanigans and my attitude, but I can tell when she's trying to make a point and get me to understand something. Her fear of the Regent is warranted, and her weariness of this particular Jarl is concerning—I tuck my curiosity away for now. This isn't about my comfort. I need to wake up and begin thinking beyond myself. It's amazing that just her tone alone can make me smarten up like this.

While I see her point and understand the path, or lack thereof, it's inevitable that I'll still whine the entire way there-it is in my nature to tease and annoy my mother after all. Once my father was gone, someone had to take the torch and keep his legacy alive. With a swish of my hair and an, "I've shown her" attitude, I swing myself onto my horse and shove another pastry in my mouth. This will be a long ride but at least I have some strawberry goodness to support me along the way.

The woods we travel through start as soon as we cross the town lines of Huginnstead, and don't end until we take a step inside a building in Lakewood itself. On the brightside, the trees will be an excellent cover while we camp tonight, although we will have to be on the watch for any creatures stalking in the darkness. I've heard enough tales to warrant an appropriate amount of fear of the forests of Asvalda, so

I'm grateful knowing my family has taught me as much as any soldier in the royal army. I may whine like a small babe, but I know how to wield a sword better than most men, as well as hit any moving mark with a bow and arrow.

Weapons aside, I'm also constantly practicing my magic as we ride. Mother has been giving me small goals to achieve as we go; things like setting one single leaf on fire without burning the entire tree, and summoning very specific wildflowers to appear in my hand without looking at them lining the forest's trail. So far, I've done everything within the first three tries, something she has reminds me numerous times should not be possible—with herself as the exception.

Knowing, and seemingly also not knowing, the dangers that we will soon face has me eager to practice the more tactical forms of magic. I slow my horse to let Mother get significantly ahead of me, still in sight, and manage to force the dagger strapped to her hip fly toward me, manipulating it mid-air to assure it reaches my outstretched hand and not my skull. Or my horse's for that matter.

Unamused but unwilling to hide her pride, Mother summons her dagger back and gives me more miniscule tasks in order to better hone the finer skills of my magic, like a small child practicing with small objects. I quickly become grateful for her assignments when I'm able to stop a hawk mid-air so that a poor rabbit it was hunting could escape a gruesome end. The hawk stays frozen in the air, completely unmoving, until I shift my body forward once more—deciding the rabbit has gotten enough of a head start.

"Let us hope no one stops us from eating our dinner as you just did to that hawk." Mother says while turning her head to look at me.

"How did you even see what I just did? There were no sounds to be heard."

"Exactly daughter." She says, facing forward once again. She raises a hand with her pointer finger out as if to scold me. "There was a barely audible movement of wings and then suddenly nothing. There should have been an animal's screech of pain, rustling leaves while it soared back into the sky, but there was nothing at all."

She makes a fair point, something I wouldn't have thought of on my own.

"Next, I will have you practice hearing the space around you, and with your eyes closed, you will tell me exactly what the animals around us are doing. You should learn how to use your magic as a second set of eyes. You will catch many things behind your back in that manner."

Well that explains how she always knew I was making faces behind her as a child, and when I would try sneaking treats when she was facing away from me. Nothing ever got past this woman and now I'll finally learn how she did it.

To begin, I close my eyes and focus on all of the smaller noises that are usually just in the background going unnoticed. I hear small claws of a squirrel lightly puncturing dried bark on the third tree to my left as it climbs to its desired branch. Numerous bugs fly around a long dead animal—I sense about fourteen of them, buzzing and landing on the decaying fur. The hawk I thwarted before is up above the tree cover, soaring past repeatedly, looking for another small creature to capture.

The song of wind and water takes hold of my senses, gentle music from a string instrument intertwined with nature's tune. This strikes me as odd as there are no rivers or ponds for some ways and there is surely no civilization anywhere near us, we are far enough away from Huginnstead for any festivities to be heard from here.

The trickling water becomes steadily more harsh, completely overpowering my senses. The power of the music fills my body. I feel lighter, happier than ever before. It pains my body not to set myself free to the tune—I need to find the source of the woodland song, I need to dance and sing with it, surely that is much more important than anything else in this moment, I-

Caw, Caw.

A shadow of black swoops past, forcing a gust of air into my face and breaking me out of my trance. After refocusing my eyes, I spot a raven sitting on my mother's knee; she looks down at him like they are having a silent conversation. A soft clicking noise alerts me to the second raven taking a stance on my shoulder. It looks at me with strangely human eyes, I know that he's trying to make sure I am completely snapped out of whatever magic had my mind trapped. Extending my hand out to him, he hops on and wraps his long toes around my fingers.

"Thank you, sir raven. It appears you have given me warning once again."

He turns his head, calling to the other bird; and with that, they fly away once more. My mother's horse slows until we ride side by side.

"He spoke to me—the raven did," she practically whispers. "He told me to be wary of the songs in the wind. There are stronger threats among these trees than we thought."

I nod in understanding, nervous as to what would have happened if I had followed the music I heard, danced with it as I ached for. We decide it is best if I hold off on practicing my magic with only my senses for a bit and instead we ride in silence for another few hours. As soon as the sky is shaded in orange, we make camp and divide rations between us.

Deciding to take my first watch once the sky turns dark, I sit with Frey by our shelter and try manipulating the flame of our fire to dance in odd ways. Soft sounds of small feet scurrying through moss and fallen branches continue to keep me on edge, so I try using amplified senses once more in order to keep a better metaphorical eye out in the night.

This time as I close my eyes, the fire sounds as if it is roaring. It masks the other sounds of the forest, so I push the noise into a box in my mind to mute the crackling flames, and I allow all of the other noises in the night to come flooding in.

SEVENTEEN
BREE

Wake up! Wake up!
Before it can sup!
It snuck in her mind,
With the music it binds.
Wake up, dear mother,
There is not much time!
It will lure her in,
Before breaking her spine.
WAKE UP!

I rush out of the tent so quickly that I almost take the entire thing with me as I tumble out of the opening. I was woken by the rhyming ravens, working overtime by warning us of danger once again. Except it seems this time the danger found my daughter before I could stop it.

In order to find her I need to steady my breaths, close my eyes, and do as I instructed her earlier in the day. I don't hear the music she claimed was singing to her mere hours ago, but I can hear it now-off in the distance.

She did not go far,
Just follow the stars.

But do make haste,
Before it's too late!

Looking up, it is impossible to see the stars. The tree cover is too thick, it is unbelievable we could even see daylight when the sun was up. The raven wouldn't tell me to follow the stars for no reason, there must be another way.

Nan once told me stories of playful stars that would keep her company when the King and Queen were busy or traveling without her. She had no siblings or cousins, and there were no children around her age for years. She would lay in the grass in the castle gardens and close her eyes. She prayed to the gods that someone could be with her, play with her, guide her while her parents were away.

One night, the stars took pity on her after laying there night after night, lonely as can be and whispered to her in the night. She said that their voices sounded like sparkles of fairy dust, dancing and twirling through the breeze.

This is the best plan I can come up with, rather than aimlessly running through the woods trying to track down the music that sounds as if it is coming from every direction. So I steady myself against a tree, slow my breath once again, and close my eyes. I pray, not to the gods, but to the stars directly. I tell them of our plans and of our bloodline, though they surely know already. I give them promises of a fair world and peace when I sit on the throne. I promise to sit beneath them every night for the rest of my days in thanks and devotion.

I silently plead for my daughter to be unharmed and come back to me.

I beg for them to guide me to her, for I cannot lose another. I refuse to lose my daughter most of all. She is everything, not only to me but to the future of this kingdom.

I beg.

"Please..." I croak, holding a sob that has built up no matter how much I focus. "Please help me find her..."

I never knew that the act of glowing in the darkness would have a sound, and yet I can hear it clearly. It sounds like a soft jingle of a small bell, and a quiet humming. I feel the glowing in front of me, radiating warmth and safety. I open my eyes to a trail of small floating orbs of light, forming a path—a path of stars.

Without another thought, I run.

Branches tear at my face as I race through the trees. Roots make an effort to trip me, but I use my magic to steady myself with more ability than I'd normally be able to. Mead appears by my side and runs ahead, gracefully jumping over any obstacles and making sure to get to her as quickly as possible. The sound of running water and strumming grows louder in my mind, giving me a push to run even faster–faster than a human should be capable of.

There's a clearing up ahead, just large enough to fit a small pond with a large boulder placed in the center, the top half breaking the water and acting as a seat for the creature responsible for Annie's disappearance from camp. The clearing is lit by the full moon above, no trees to block its light.

As a mother, the scene in front of me is terrifying, but knowing it is not too late has me worrying about nothing else. Annie is waist deep in the pond that doesn't even seem like it should be able to even rise to her navel, let alone any deeper-yet she continues to slowly move forward. She's in a trance, moving her arms around her as if she is dancing with someone; she does not remove her gaze from the creature on the boulder.

His skin is so pale that it's translucent, the soaking black tangles of hair dangling over his shoulders making it even more so. Twigs and seaweed weave through the roots of his matted locks and beetles scurry across the sharp tips of his teeth, visible under his unnaturally wide smile, covering more than half of his face. He stares at Annie with black, soulless eyes as he plays a fiddle masterfully.

Never in my travels have I encountered a fossegrim, but I do know that he should not be trying to drown a woman without provocation–there's something horribly off about this. A small pair of eyes shines in the moonlight across the pond, glaring at the fossegrim's back. The cat pounces onto the boulder and attacks the grim from behind, ending his song and stopping Annie in her tracks, right as her nose hovers above the water, seconds away from being submerged. Deep growling and hissing comes from the pair as they fall into the water, giving me the opportunity to pull Annie out.

Entering the pond, I realize there is dark magic at play. I'm standing directly behind my daughter, her chest still submerged and yet I'm only ankle deep. There is no sudden drop off and no explanation as for why she is so much deeper than I. When she stood here moments ago, she was neck deep. Even now, as I pull her from the neckline of her tunic, her entire body is beneath the pond until I drag her completely out. As soon there is no other part of her body in the enchanted pond, she snaps out of her trance and begins hyperventilating.

I brush back her wet hair and hold her too—pale face against my chest, slowly rocking her back and forth as I watch the struggle beneath the water come to a close. Where there was just frothing water and large splashes seconds ago, there is now an eerie stillness as the pond turns to obsidian, trapping my dear Mead underneath.

"Mead, come."

Still sopping wet, much like my daughter, the black cat saunters toward us after walking out of the solid obsidian like it was still liquified. Once he sits beside me, the obsidian begins to shatter. It cracks and splinters until it is a heap of black shards, shooting up into the night sky and disappearing beyond the stars.

"What-what was—" Annie shivers uncontrollably, barely able to string her sentence together "—What was it?" She finally stammers out. Frey appears and nuzzles into her lap, trying to warm her.

"It appeared to us as a fossegrim, a water spirit commonly known to be excellent with string instruments. It's said their music can make anything dance, and dance you did. Although that does not explain its behavior, the pond appeared to be shallow and yet you were almost completely submerged, and whatever just happened afterwards with Mead."

A quick flap of wings signals us to our new companions. The ravens appear from the sky and land on the boulder that still remains in the middle of the clearing. They stare at us, and Mead looks at them, completely unbothered. They take turns saying each line of their rhyme, their beaks unmoving but I can tell a difference in their voices now.

The grim was no grim,
As you so wisely know.
He's a creature of magic,
Born one day ago.

He studies the monsters,
And makes them his own.
Tries to use even us,
To defeat all his foes.

He knows no location,
Of where you may be.
So he planted these creatures,

In hopes to kill thee.

Beware of the forest,
And lore you may know.
For the tales you've been taught,
You can no longer trow.

They simultaneously dip their heads in a bow and fly away.

"They've grown on me, those two."

"Aye, they have definitely proven to be helpful. You were right, they must be here to protect us. They woke me when you were taken by the magic and told me how to find you." We both stare at the spot where the ravens just stood, going through everything that just happened in the last hour and mentally preparing to find our way back to camp.

With a final stroke of her hair, I help her stand and we follow the floating stars that remain to help us find our way. The way back feels twice as long as before. When we find camp, we agree that we are done with our attempts to sleep, and we sit by the fire until morning comes.

As soon as dawn breaks, we pack up our horses and begin the rest of the journey toward Lakewood. We should make it before nightfall since we have such an early start, as well as motivation to not camp in this forest again if we're able to avoid it.

We ride down the same path as the day before, Annie wrapped in a wool blanket atop her horse with Frey tight in her arms, never seeming to lose the chill from the pond water. I look at her back and it hits me how close I was to losing everything—so soon in this journey. There will no doubt be many hardships to face before even reaching the Regent, and they will continue to try to kill us both.

I vow that will never come to fruition. We will make it to the end, and if the end decides it is taking me with it, fine, but nothing will take her. I will breathe my last breath making sure of it.

EIGHTEEN
BREE

The arrival into Lakewood is nothing like Huginnstead. This is a much smaller community, so they're not nearly as welcoming to outsiders. That isn't to say there aren't friendly or welcoming people here, it's just incredibly unsettling.

When we pass, people stop in their tracks and watch us until we are out of their line of sight. Some have noticeable disgust written across their features, others look utterly indifferent. We find a small area of the town that has a line of tiny log cabins prepared for travelers who need lodgings. They each have large evergreen trees between them for some semblance of privacy, but the cabins are still rather close too together for my liking, especially when it feels as if we can't trust anyone here. I'm wondering if we should just camp in the woods instead, but I'll take gossiping, grumpy villagers over dark-touched fae folk.

As we walk into the front door of the largest cabin with a sign out front, we are met with instant warmth. The woman who runs the unique Inn had a fire prepared a short time before we arrived in hopes of business, and we are happy to oblige. She takes payment and walks us over to where we'll stay for the night, at least the person in charge of our shelter seems nice enough.

As Annie draws herself a warm bath to finally regain her heat from last night, I prepare my map and notes on the table to take a look at our next steps. So far, I have failed to divulge a large part of my plan to anyone—including Annie. Most people would tell me I am a fool for thinking that I can accomplish this particular venture, but I would simply remind them of who I am. A Gods-blessed woman researching every avenue available to protect her family and her kingdom.

I hold my worn out notes by the candlelight, going over every little detail I can muster, even knowing that I have read these words hundreds of times. I am confident I can find these legendary weapons I've researched, but it still doesn't stop me from reading about them over and over again. I need to tell Annie about this extra adventure because we are nearing the suspected location of the first one, and she needs to be prepared.

I can't help but fear the extra risks that we will need to take in order for this to work. They won't be easy to find, and much less easy to acquire. The Gods would have made sure of that.

"Mother?" Annie calls from the bath. "Do you mind if I stay here a little longer while you get us some food? I don't think I can bear being around people tonight. I'm absolutely exhausted."

Smiling to myself, I agree. "I suppose I can go alone. I'll be back shortly, dear. Remember to keep your wits about you while I'm gone." In response, Frey appears by one of the windows as a look out while she's relaxing. Excellent idea, I'll have Mead join guard.

If I'm being honest with myself, I'm glad she wishes to stay in tonight. I need to calm myself further since our experience last night, and I'm sure Annie appreciates the alone time as well. My fear needs Annie to stay in my sight, but my trust in her abilities allows me to get a much needed break—it helps that there are two furry creatures keeping watch for us. I'm grateful for the walk, the quiet air around me outside always quiets my rushing thoughts.

There are so many factors that I still have to understand. Such as the mysterious ravens that keep appearing to save the day. I'm incredibly grateful for their protection thus far, but who are they? Where do they hail from? Why did I feel unwavering trust in them the second I met them? I even warned Annie not to give her trust too easily before we left home, and here I am, willing to rely on these ravens without a second thought.

A chill gust of wind slashes through the air, causing me to pull the knit shawl I brought tightly around my shoulders. The walk to the nearest pub is quick. I only have to pass by a couple of miserable looking villagers, but the soothing sounds of night in the trees makes up for it.

On the outside, Lakewood radiates with the peaceful nature all around the town. The same is not to be said for the inside of this establishment, as I am met with nothing but malicious glares and cold shoulders. The best I can hope for at this point is that they don't spit in our food.

As I approach the bar, the men sitting there lean away from me as though I will spread disease to them if I get too close. Their lips curl, baring their teeth like rabid dogs while the fire from the nearby hearth embellishes the rage in their eyes. The barmaid looks slightly less disgruntled, so I take my chances with her.

"Who're you?" She practically spits the words at me.

Okay, so not friendly then.

"My name is Bree. I'm just passing through town with my daughter and am hoping I can pay for a couple of warm meals here? It's the only place open at this hour." I keep my voice as pleasant as possible despite her venomous tone.

She contemplates my words, eyebrows scrunched together and eyes squinted. "Don't have much this late. Yer gonna have to deal with the leftover soup nobody wanted and a couple of cold turkey legs—that is, if the cook didn't toss 'em already."

The men on either side of me snicker under their breaths, the rage in their glares being replaced with mockery.

"I'll take whatever you have, thank you dearly."

She scoffs at my words, rolls her eyes so dramatically I'm surprised they don't roll right out of her head, and turns to stalk back into the kitchen.

As I stand there waiting for my "meal" I can feel the air change around me. The patrons are suddenly more confident—eagerly awaiting the perfect opportunity to shame me for something, I'm sure. The men at the bar continue to snicker amongst themselves as the barmaid shouts obscenities in the kitchen. Other men that are seated in booths against the back wall directly behind me scoot out of their seats and slowly walk toward me.

They have no idea that I can sense them while facing the opposite direction. I don't dare move my hand toward the hidden dagger on my waistline—men like this would take the threat and end it immediately.

The man who approaches me from behind has long hair that reaches past his elbows, the pigment matching that of the fire in the hearth. His full beard completely covers the bottom half of his face, leaving only his knob of a nose and dark eyes visible. He holds a pint of ale in one hand and reaches behind his back with the other. His movements make me change my mind about my dagger, and turn to face him just as his path is interrupted by two tall, slender men. I can only see the back of them, but they both stand in front of my would-be assailant with spines straight and chests out.

"Hmm...a man with no manners is no man at all."

"Threatening a woman? Who has the gall?"

The hair on my arms rises immediately at the familiar voices spitting their rhymes. Their human voices sound exactly like the ones that came from the ravens when they were reciting their poetic warnings.

But there is no possible way these men are the ravens—what kind of magic would they have to possess to do such a thing? The only beings who hold such magic, besides my family, are the Gods and the Regent.

"The fuck are you two saying?" The man gruffly demands of the men. His brows look more like fluffy orange caterpillars than ever as they crinkle in confusion on his forehead.

"Her back was turned, yet you approach..."

"For nothing more but to hurt and poach."

As I finally turn to face the three men, I notice the rest of the crowd in here stops pretending to have conversations with each other—they are all now blatantly staring at the scene playing out before them. The women quietly blink from the burly man to the apparent twins; the men amongst them assess their body language to determine whether they should step in or not.

The twins before me both wear pure white tunics that are nicely tucked into wrinkle-free black trousers. Their sleeves are rolled up to their elbows, showcasing elaborate designs on their skin that I can't make sense of, but also cannot deny their beauty. Their hair is as black and sleek as their raven feathers and they stand with daring confidence in front of the man that's twice their size.

The red-haired man—who looks much larger now that I see him with my eyes rather than senses—lifts his arm above his head as if to hit the two protecting me, yet he stops it in mid-air.

Actually, it seems the entire room has gone completely still besides myself and the men as they turn around to finally face me. My eyes widen in shock and my eyebrows practically touch my hairline as I realize that these are not men at all, they seem to be barely adults–Annie's age at the most.

The only difference between the two of them is the color of their eyes and the style of their hair. The one to my right has irises so magical,

I would believe it if he told me they were made from aquamarine—a blue that holds the ocean waves in its grasp.

The other has eyes of pure fluorite. The purple and turquoise fade into each other the same as the crystal itself. The eyes of these mysterious raven males are nothing short of mesmerizing and magical. Freckles lightly spread across their cheeks and bridge of their noses. Fluorite eyes has his hair all over the place, a complete mess that somehow does not dissuade from his otherwise classy attire. Aquamarine's hair swoops in the front, long enough that if it laid flat it would certainly tangle in his eyelashes.

While taking in their appearance, I realize that there is something more to our connection that I originally thought. In their raven forms, it was clear they were on our side. In their human forms however, it is *undeniable* that I somehow know these two without ever having met them before. They are my home, they are important, and they are trustworthy.

"Our favorite Ragna out to play!" Aquamarine sings with a voice deeper than one would expect from a male with his stature.

"She wanders alone in the absence of day!"

"Does she learn nothing, dear brother?"

"Apparently, she's just like her mother."

"I am *nothing* like Tessa." I challenge the insult, my words spitting in disrespect. "She fled at the first sign of danger and never looked back. I would never leave my family behind, my daughter especially."

Whatever sense of familiarity I have found in these boys, I immediately push away with my irritation at their words. Wandering around at night to get a meal for us cannot possibly be comparable to Tessa leaving us all without a word of where she was going or why.

She could be captured and you know this.

Ungrateful, uncaring daughter.

"Your anger deceives you, if only you knew..."

"All of the things your mother goes through."

Someone submerges me into the frozen lake, for nothing else could explain the frigid fear that courses through my blood. It turns my skin ice cold and slows the blood in my veins—surely she ran from us and she's fine, living in hiding while safe and protected.

Right?

Pa and I have always been aware of the possibility that something horrible could have happened to her, but we never encountered any kind of confirmation or hint as to what life has been like for her these past years. That is, until these mysterious boys appeared.

"What do you know of my mother? Where is she?" I frantically ask, ready to beg at this point.

Pity transforms their countenance, the slight smirk they once wore now slants downward, their brows creasing into worry. Rather than taking turns in their rhymes and riddles, they now speak together.

"Time for fear is not yet here,

Worry more for what comes near.

These foolish men will leave you be,

Just leave here soon or face their greed.

When it is time, she will appear,

Then you will know to face your fear.

Until the day, just watch the skies,

We will be near so no one dies."

They each take one of my hands and squeeze. They say nothing more, but I can feel all of what they have left unsaid in their grasp. They will always be here to protect us, and while they obviously know more information than they are telling me, they are still giving me hope and answers that I never expected to gain.

They release my hands simultaneously and within a heartbeat they transform into their raven forms once again. Before flying out of the open door, I rush to stop them.

"Wait! What are your names? Why are you helping us?"

They can only speak into my mind now as they respond, quite unsurprisingly, with another poem to make me question everything I know.

His magic runs deep,
His interests do span.
He wants you safe,
And who better to send?
Aeven and Elvind come to your stead.
He sires our power,
But so does another.
You know her well,
And her story will tell.
Farewell, sweet Bree.
Snatch thy food,
return to safety.

They fly out of the pub, leaving me reeling. Deciding to wait to go over all of their words until I can replay the scene to Annie, I turn to see the barmaid had frozen halfway through the doorway with our food when the boys stopped time. I jump over the bar to quickly grab our dinner before everyone snaps back to normal, and the giant man decides he still wants to flatten me into the floor.

Walking back to the Inn, all I can think to myself is what in the *Hels* just happened here tonight?

NINETEEN

ANNIE

Apparently, Mother had an interesting night. I got out of the bath and fell asleep almost immediately after she left to get us dinner. I woke slightly when she returned, but even the smell of fresh food wasn't enough to keep my eyes open. She let me sleep through the night, but I could tell as soon as I woke up that the gears were turning rapidly in her mind.

Even now, as she's packing up the few things from the night while I eat my cold dinner for breakfast, she's quiet and contemplating. She even went to restock all of our supplies in town by herself this morning. Whatever happened on her little adventure has her seriously deep in her thoughts and I can't help but be incredibly curious.

"Is something wrong?" I ask before gnawing on the hardened bread, trying to break a piece off.

She stops in the middle of packing the neatly folded night shirt she wore back into her bag. "The ravens. They—they aren't really ravens," she answered uncertainly.

"Well I could've told you that." I set down the rock of bread to focus on her new information, ready to learn about our feathery friends. "I'm assuming you found out what they actually are? Did you see them last night?"

Placing both of her hands neatly on top of her bag, her eyes seem to be looking far away, not focusing on anything in particular as she fidgets with the wedding ring on her finger. With a deep breath, she finally tells me of her night and all that transpired. She tells me of the angry patrons, that the ravens—who are called Aeven and Elvind—and how they protected her and revealed small snippets of secrets.

My food threatens to come back up when she informs me that my grandmother *is* alive and may not be staying away from us on her own accord. That would mean she's most likely being held against her will and tortured. The thought burns my eyes and sours my stomach further. I cannot imagine the guilt my mother must be feeling. For years she has been convinced that Tessa abandoned us when she never came back. To find out that we should have been looking for her this entire time...I set down my plate and stand by Mother. Mistakes have been made, but we worked with what little information we had.

"Pa is going to be so heartbroken...he knew that we should have tried harder to find her. He told me so himself." My mother practically whispers, making me have to stop what I'm doing in order to hear her. "He won't survive this Annie...he'll be so defeated."

I grab her hands tightly, sending resilience through our connection. "Well then, we'll just have to soften the blow by presenting his daughter to him at the same time as telling him. It won't cure the guilt but at least he'll finally see her safety with his own eyes. You said before that you two had a theory that this was possible, so it won't completely blind side him."

"We have so much more to accomplish now. Finding her not only just saves a member of our family when we have already lost too many, but it also takes away a weapon that could potentially be used against us. Why keep her alive this long if she can give no further information or be of further use to them? I'm willing to bet that the Regent knew someone would eventually venture out of the safety of our home to find her."

We work in silence as we pack up the rest of our belongings quickly to get a head start on our day. Adding another agenda to this budding adventure has only added a tense level of uncertainty between the two of us. There's no question that we need to find and help Tessa as soon as we possibly can, but we also need to keep to the plan. Uncle Jaris is expecting us and too much delay could ruin everything. Together, we come to the conclusion that if anyone could begin to point us in the right direction as to her whereabouts and also provide reinforcements, it would be the man behind the military.

After a couple of hours riding in silence, I can't take it anymore. The skin of my wrist is becoming raw from my constant fidgeting and rubbing in my anxiety. There are certain holes in this plan that I need answers to.

"You mentioned Tessa being used as a weapon against us earlier, but what weapons do we currently possess against the Regent besides our magic? If it were enough to rely solely on two mortals with some fancy tricks to lead an army then this should be simple." The end of my statement earns a hard look from my mother. I'm surprised her neck doesn't crack from the sudden forceful way in which she turns to glare into my very soul. "Before you even go on about it, I'm not naive to the dangers ahead of us and the threat that is posed by this man. I'm simply curious about whatever it is that you inevitably have hidden up your sleeve to truly help our side of the war."

With a disgruntled huff and a shake of her head, she turns forward once again in silence rather than answering me.

"You do have a course of action planned against him besides just the army, right?" When she continues not to answer, I squeeze my heels against the sides of my steed until our horses are side by side. "I realize that your mother has been held captive for about eighteen years but I do think she would have taught you that ignoring people is rude before she was gone, no?"

She pulls the reins to her horse and comes to an abrupt stop, her face emotionless while also clearly harboring immense frustration mixed with...do I sense guilt? Her shoulders draw up, and her elbows tuck tightly to her sides.

Her chin quivers as she speaks, "I realize that we tend to have very informal banter than a mother and daughter typically would, but let me remind you that I *am* in fact your mother and that maybe there is a *reason* for my silence." She makes eye contact with me and turns her head so slightly, I could be convinced it was just the wind in her hair. "Your snarky comments are unnecessary even if I am being rude by not answering your questions."

"Well, I appreciate that you *recognize* that you were being rude so I'm sorry that I upset you. On the other hand, you had to have expected unrelenting questions throughout this journey, I mean, we *are* uprooting our entire lives for this and could very well *die*. I just want to understand more of what you have planned and what I have prepared my life for."

Her face falls into a softer gaze, almost mournful, as she pushes ahead once again and we continue down the path. The emotions flitting across her face in the last few moments leave me pondering what her actual plan is even more than before.

She takes a deep breath, and when she exhales her lips quiver, "There are legends of weapons created for the Gods that are hidden in Asvalda, waiting to be used in future battles against their enemies."

Divine weapons? That is the last thing I was expecting to hear.

"They are supposedly hidden where only the Gods themselves can find them, as they are the ones who chose their homes. I, along with Jaris, have researched these legends relentlessly over the years. It was brought to his attention by Nan before she had decided to stay hidden rather than take back the throne. He worked with Tessa to find them as well." She speaks so quietly that I practically fall off my horse trying to hear her properly.

"My plan has always included looking for two of these weapons to help aid us in battle against the Regent. They have many stories attached to them, as they have already been used by Thor and Odin themselves. They are known as Mjölnir and Gungnir, and Jaris thinks he knows the location of both."

Well, that certainly changes things. She used to tell me stories with the weapons making an appearance when I was young, and they fascinated me. Mjölnir and Gungnir were made by dwarves in another realm; their power is said to be unsurpassable. It also just so happens that my favorite tale of Thor and Loki dressing as ladies was to retrieve Mjölnir.

"Does Pa know about this?"

"He does not, by request of Uncle Jaris. He was worried that Pa would try to convince him and Tessa to stop their research. As it could prove either impossible, or too dangerous. He would have been right of course, for it is not as simple as merely finding and using the hammer and spear."

"Do you know where they're hidden? If the Gods made sure to keep them safe then what makes you think we will be able to find them ourselves? I bet I can guess what your answer will be, 'Because we are blessed by those Gods, Annie.'" I can't help that my eyes roll as I impersonate her, it seems as though that has been the answer to *everything* without actually giving us any tangible evidence. I catch myself rubbing the sore skin of my wrist again and summon Frey to keep my hands busy. He also serves to keep my hands warm, the temperature continues to drop the closer we get to the barren land.

"All of this *is* because we are blessed by the Gods. You may get tired of hearing it, in which case you must get over that hurdle. Their choice was not made lightly, the entire Kingdom is even named after our family. We are *meant* to be on that throne and the Gods will allow us to do impossible things in order to reclaim it." Her words are laced with frustration, knuckles white as they grip the reins too tightly. She maintains a heavy silence for a few tense moments before she continues.

"As I said, it is not as simple as just finding the weapons. There are two artifacts that accompany Mjölnir in the stories, the Gauntlets of Thor and the Belt of Megin. If either of us attempted to *wield* Mjölnir without the safety of Thor's iron gloves, we would perish immediately. The raw power infused into the weapon is too much for any mortal to bear, unless one has the Gauntlets."

This catches my attention, Mjölnir is as famous as the Gods themselves, but not much is known about Thor's gloves and belt. I haven't realized that there was more to the use of the divine hammer than simply wielding it.

"And the Belt of Megin?" I ask, intrigued.

"It is not necessary in the same way the Gauntlets are. It is said that whoever wears the belt of woven iron imbues the strength of Thor himself. The God's strength even doubles when he is the one wearing them. It may not be necessary in order to use the hammer in battle, but the foes we are up against are mighty and we will need every single advantage we can get. Uncle Jaris and I suspect that the two artifacts may be hidden together but separate from Mjölnir."

"Okay, so to make sure I am understanding this correctly—we have to first find the Gauntlets of Thor and then we can hunt for Mjölnir? Where do you think they are?" Everything about this new addition to our quest is making my head spin. We go from traveling to our Uncle for support, to hunting for legendary weapons on the way.

Simple, really.

I clutch my head between my fingers, attempting to massage out the headache this cluster of information is causing.

"It doesn't matter which we find first, as long as Mjölnir is not wielded in battle, it will not harm us, but the gloves must be found before we encounter the Regent."

"Oh yes—that is all! 'Tis as easy as baking bread I would imagine."

My mother only scoffs in response to my hysterics. She has had much more time to process everything, and I suspect she finds amusement in my reactions now since I spy a slight smirk on her face.

"Simmer down, little one. Do not let your worry take over your mind before we're even faced with the task. Besides, we'll be tracking down Gungnir first, I believe I've found its location. Uncle Jaris is in charge of figuring out where Mjölnir is."

"He didn't tell you where it is yet?"

"Goodness no, we kept our respective research to ourselves to ensure the information does not fall into anyone else's hands by including anything in letters. As far as we know, no one has ever had reason to attempt finding the weapons and we would like to keep it that way."

Yes, well, no one has ever had to steal back their throne from an evil demi-god with black magic and eternal youth until now...

PART THREE

TWENTY

ANNIE

The Frostreik is by far my least favorite place in this Gods-forsaken world. Last night, we set up camp on the outskirts of the snowy landscape, where the area tormented us. Even with magic to get rid of the snow and thaw the frozen ground, it was too cold and far too miserable. The weather had no interest in our fire, suffocating it with heavy blankets of snow every time we attempted to light another. Mother had to teach me how to use magic to warm myself and my food, but to use it sparingly to avoid draining myself too quickly. We would need this skill throughout the entire trek through this Hel.

Traveling through The Frostreik is typically only attempted by hunters who try to capture the legendary monster who roams the land; making the notion that we'll make it through here absolutely absurd. It's important to note that these hunters have been raised in nearby areas and have significantly more knowledge on snow walking than two women from an island, one of which has never even *seen* snow until now. Mother said that she picked up the ability to walk through deep snow quite swiftly when she visited Uncle Jaris once as a child, and suspects that I will do just as well.

As we finish packing up camp, we are met with a flurry of white at the edge of the forest path, creating a solid barrier from one climate to another. The storms that possess the land here are infamous across Asvalda, as they are so fierce, that many have not come out the other side by Frostfjord, forever lost in a sea of snow. There's no gradual temperature change closer to the barrier. I put my hand through it, and am instantly met with a biting cold, mentally taking back my previous insults to the forest side.

I gasp in shock as I pull my hand back and cradle it against my chest in an effort to regain its warmth. I can sense Mother watching me, gauging my reaction and waiting for an accusation she knows is coming.

"The Frostreik has magic, it dominates the air. You did not bring us here for a stealthier route to Frostheim, there is something here." I turn to face her, the first ounce of fear filling my lungs as I breathe for the first time since the woodland song.

"Land cannot have its own magic. It's a creature that controls the weather of The Frostreik—a deity, in the stories often told in these parts." She stares into the wall of snow like she can see through it clearly, like she sees her destination within reach. The air around us is eerily calm, only adding to the fear that overtakes me.

"What is a deity doing in the mortal realm?" I ask, my voice barely above a whisper.

Her eyes break away from whatever they saw as she steadily turns only her head to look at me once more. "The Gods do not leave behind treasures without protection, Annie." Without another word, she climbs onto her horse, and motions for me to do the same. Together, we march forward through the barrier of snow and ice.

The way through The Frostreik, thus far, has been nothing short of exhausting. In order to protect our horses from the elements, we cast warmth charms over the lot of us—while simultaneously hardening the ground as they walk in order to stop them from sinking down to their bellies in the snow.

The winds are fierce as they scream through the sky, circling us as we go. The thick fur-lined hood pulled around my face does the bare minimum of keeping my skin from being pelted by the harsh hail that has gotten gradually worse the further we go. Our horses choose to walk as close together as they can, causing my legs to occasionally bump my mother's. They fear the air as I do and they seek each other for comfort, nudging the neck of the other when the wind is particularly aggressive to keep themselves going.

If it weren't for the proximity of our steeds, there would be nothing to ensure that my mother was still with me at all. Several times, I've held my hand inches from my face and could only see a faint shadow of where it should be. Thick flurries of the storm whip around us—trapping us amongst a blank canvas.

It is impossible to tell how long we have been traveling. It seems that even the sky is not allowed to sleep, constantly blanketed in the glacial white. I can only hope that the incredible directional skills my mother has always garnered is steering us in the right direction. She gave no further explanation, but I can only assume that this is where we'll find Gungnir. Why else would a mythical deity curse the grounds in their apparent protection?

The entire thing makes me wonder how any hunters make it out here, for they have no way of getting animals through, or manifesting a seedling of extra warmth like we do. It's no wonder no one has ever caught the legendary monster they so greatly fear, it would be impossible for them to make it as far as we have without leaving the safer trail to Frostfjord.

After a handful of hours stuck in my own thoughts, Mother finally squeezes my knee to gain my attention. Our horses stop in their tracks and I can feel rather than see her jump from her horse and begin to set up for some rest. Once I get my last bag off of the saddle, both animals begin quickly trotting toward something I cannot see, so close together their wide bellies touch as they go. I sense the warmth of Mother beside me, and can finally make out her features. Only, the features that grace her face are those of terror. Her eyes are practically bulging from her face, and her mouth hangs slightly open, the corners dipping downward. Looking back in the direction our horses were last seen, I can only see a blanket of white. The winds howl louder than ever, but just beneath the bellows of The Frostreik is the distinct sound of one horse's whinny, and another's roar of distress.

My eyes snap back to my mother whose mask of horror mirrors my own. In unspoken understanding, we turn together, hand in hand, and run.

Without time to secure our wooden shoes with fanned woven soles for easier travel across the snow, we're forced to rely on magic alone. My mother and I may be naturally attuned to using it, but we're already dangerously close to exhaustion after helping our horses trudge through the landscape, and we cannot afford to fall to the same fate as our hooved companions.

Still unaware of what exactly we're running from, I attempt to glance behind me, spotting nothing but the exact scene that's been present since we crossed the barrier into this horrid land—white.

All I can hear are the labored breaths tearing through my chest and the crunch of the solidified snow beneath our feet. I want to scream to Mother, I need to know what she saw, but other than my ragged breaths, there's only the sound of continued wails from the tempestuous storm that will swallow my words with ease. She tugs my arm forward again to look straight ahead.

Right, I need to focus on the endless cycle necessary for our escape: imagine the balls of light beneath my feet, harden the snow, push forward, steady myself, repeat. My mother can complete the steps much quicker than I, but she slows herself as to not pull and make me lose my balance. I can tell that she's doing her best to keep me going as I push my magic as far as I possibly can–more than I have had to do all at once up to this point. My energy is draining, my magic is sucking the life out of me. My skin heats enough to melt snow before it even touches my skin, boiling the blood within my veins. My body is threatening to give out, welcoming the burn out of magic.

My mother looks as if she's going through similar pain. Steam surrounds her body from her body heat, her face redder than an apple. The panic in her steps can barely be seen, but I know it is there. It's the way she squeezes my hand while we run, the way she pulls me to her side when she hears a sound I am deaf to. Above all, it radiates from her very soul and touches mine—for she panics for my life and I've only felt her fear like this once before.

Focus, Annie, of course she is scared.

Focus, Annalysa.

My steps falter and I stumble in surprise from the intrusion into my thoughts. What in the Nine Realms was that?

It's herding you toward its home. Brace yourself.

"What are the Gods playing at? Do you hear him?" I scream to Mother, willing her to hear me above the sounds of the weather. She crouches down in front of me. Her hands crush my shoulders, shaking me to get my attention. When did I end up on the ground? She's clearly screaming something at me but I cannot hear her, though she's so close that I can feel the heat from her breath on my face.

I scramble to my feet and allow her to pull me forward once more. I still can't hear her words, but I *do* hear a much more ominous noise–an agonized howl of pain from a man. Mother hears it too, and it causes her pause even amongst her motherly instincts to rush me to safety. The man continues to yell and it sounds so familiar, like I've heard it before.

We come to a full stop, completely enthralled by the screaming. A shuddering sob sounds beside me and as I turn to find the source, I'm faced with a look that I haven't seen in thirteen years. Earth shattering heartbreak possesses my mother's entire being and she frantically searches through the blizzard for the source. Within a fraction of a second, everything stops. The wind becomes silent and seems to freeze mid-air. Even the stray hairs that escaped my hood no longer whip across my face.

Once again, the only sounds that can be heard are the heavy breaths from my mother and I. We stay completely still for what feels like an eternity—waiting. My eyes are all that I dare to move, I have to try to see what is out there—what is coming. I search the entire space of white that is directly in front of me, willing something to appear for me.

Finally, in my peripheral vision, there's a shadow. I strain my eyes as much as I can, trying to make sense of the outline. It resembles a broad man, but I'm still unable to get a clear look. I take a chance, and turn my head toward the shadow slightly in order to determine who he is. The shadow seems further away, but is still more clear without the flurries of snow tearing through the wind. The man sits upon a horse with too many legs, and he holds a menacing spear in his grasp. Slowly, he raises his free hand until his arm is fully extended, pointing to his left–into the depths of The Frostreik.

I feel a similar pull to follow, the same as when I was tranced by the Grim, except this time I'm still in control of my own mind. There's an incessant tug, like an itch, urging me to go, go, go. I *need* to follow his direction. He's leading me to where we need to go.

Forgetting that I am supposed to stay still, I surge forward to begin our escape, and that's when all Hel breaks loose. Another anguished yell from the man explodes in my head, he's not just nearby, but screaming directly into my ears. The moment his scream silences again without even an echo through the air, a small whimper escapes Mother, and with it all sense of our sanity.

"Destrin…"

No. He's dead. What is this trickery?

"Mother?"

She continues her frantic search around us for her husband and doesn't hear me call for her.

"Mother, please hear me. He's gone, that isn't him. Look at me."

Heavy steps crash into the ground nearby, although the only thing to be seen are misshapen hills and white flakes scattered through the atmosphere, still stuck in their path mid-air. I take her hand and pull her against me, preparing myself to bolt forward in the direction I was guided. The man and his horse are in the same spot as before, but they seem significantly closer now. I can see details I couldn't before, like his grayed hair and a strip of leather covering one of his eyes.

"I will help you this time, I will fight with you…" She continues her crazed whispers for my father, and begins to pull away from me to try to find him. I cannot lose her in this place, it's a frozen graveyard I refuse to let us die in.

I place both of my hands around her face and force her to look at me. "Mother! Destrin is dead!" I frantically look over her face, desperate for her to come back to reality—to break whatever has a hold on her.

No consciousness can be found in her eyes, they are completely glazed over as they look through me. She's unable to get past the fact that she heard her husband's screams of pain, it's like she is in a trance of her own. This is beyond what I imagined could have happened out here. I don't have her sense of direction, my magic is not yet as precise as hers, I'll get us killed and everything we've gone through in our lives will have been for nothing. Simply because I have no idea where to start when the adult here is in distress.

No.

She would do everything in her power if our roles were switched. I need to close my mind to fear and focus on what I know. This will be close to impossible, but it's up to me to get us away from whatever is mimicking my father, nothing that sounds like the dead can be trusted.

She has stopped pulling away and allows me to position her to run with me when it's time. Looking her over to make sure she's okay, I search for the shadow to find that he's no longer there—but something else is.

Moments ago, I saw a deformed hill with jagged rocks along its crest while searching for my guide. Now, as the hill rises from the ground, shaking the earth in its wake, I realize how grave my mistake in assuming was. It's not rocks that line the top of the hill, but broken ribs and cracked vertebrae that have torn their way through black, decaying skin. It's not snow that covers the hill, but a long coat of stringy white fur, swaying in the nonexistent breeze as the "hill" rises higher and higher.

A terrifying distance away from the hunched spine that has almost completely emerged, is a set of rotted horns that begin above empty black sockets of bone where eyes were once sheltered, and curl all the way back into the matted fur of its neck. The hill has no face, nothing but jutted bones and deformed features of what was once the skull of an animal, a bear perhaps.

Two fangs protrude from the skull in a gumless grimace, each one larger than a canoe. The deity rises to its full height, so high above the ground I have no doubt it could scale the Frostheim Mountains in seconds, and it turns its head toward us, bones grinding and cracking against each other at the movement.

This giant has to be the guard of Gungnir, there's no common creature like this monstrosity anywhere even outside of Asvalda. As soon as I make the decision to run with Mother in the direction my guide pointed, the undead creature drops it's jaw with a sickening crack–putting a splitting tree to shame, and releases a supernatural howl so loud, I suddenly feel a warmth pooling in my ears and trickling down my neck as the world around me fades to black.

TWENTY-ONE
ZANDER

When a Lakelander is caught off guard by a storm in The Frostreik, it tends to cause alarm amongst the entire village of Lakewood. There hasn't been a blizzard this significant for as long as I've been alive, and owning the land closest to the frozen tundra makes me responsible for signaling any suspicious weather to the community. Abandoning the pile of wood I've been splitting all morning, I call for my wife to come outside to see this for herself.

"What is it, Zander? I have a fresh loaf almost finished baking and I–" Asa cuts herself off when her sight lands in the direction of The Frostreik.

In the last forty-five years of being married to her, I've never seen such concern etched into the lines of her face—until now. Her usual warm, wrinkled skin turns to deeper caverns across her forehead in concern, making her look twenty years older than she is. Asa's crystal blue eyes scan the sky, squinting against the bright white of the blizzard. She's so struck by the storm in the distance that she doesn't even attempt to pull back the gray strands of hair that have escaped from her braid and wrap across her face—too focused on the imminent doom that threatens us like never before.

Distant howls crack through the air, and an otherworldly screech makes us both cover our ears. Asa runs close to my side in terror, wrapping her thin arms around my waist, and I put my arm around her shoulders in return.

Only the dead make such sounds.

"I must go and warn the rest of Lakewood. Maybe someone knows what could have angered the Gods, but either way, they must prepare in case it reeks havoc here." I squeeze her shoulders and kiss her temple before heading to our small stable.

I rush through the shortest path to the main part of the village on my horse, keeping an eye out for any straggling neighbors who may be otherwise unaware. I'm used to the typical chill of Lakewood, but this new cold brings a substantial ache to my bones, and my haste makes it worse.

As I arrive in town, I notice there is already a mob of people outside of the pub, yelling accusations I cannot make out. While staying atop my horse, I push through the people in order to find the center so I can gain their attention. Whatever they're upset about can be put on hold until we can properly assess the danger looming nearby.

Further into the crowd, I can pick out more of their protests as some people grow quiet as they see me approach, and others simply get louder to get their point across. The middle of the crowd is where most of the energy is focused, people shouting over each other trying to get the attention of leadership.

"Witches!"

"...must be found and hanged!"

"They are the cause of this..."

"Someone kill those damn birds!"

"Zander! Everyone, please, move aside for Zander." The familiar voice of the Jarl rises above all others, forcing everyone to create a path wide enough for my horse to move forward.

Approaching the Jarl, I notice that he is filled with intense scrutiny, and a miniscule sliver of hope lingering beneath now that he sees me. The moment my feet touch the ground, he clasps me on the back and whispers close to my ear, "What is out there? What's happening in The Frostreik?"

The only response I can muster in his unexpected proximity is an uncertain shake of my head. The men who see my reaction quickly spread hushed, fearful words amongst their peers. If I have no answers for them, then what hope do we have of preparing properly for whatever may happen, if anything at all? Unwilling to allow the Jarl to lose control of the crowd, I adjust my posture in hopes of instilling unwavering confidence to dull the rampant nerves.

"Please, quiet down, we must help each other." The baritone of my voice penetrates the remaining fusion of shouts and whispers.

In response, all eyes land on me, ready to judge my observations for themselves. Confidence naturally comes to me when I speak to the village, but in the wake of such uncertainty, I'm met with an uneasiness that threatens to consume as I tell them the little I know. "Above The Frostreik is a storm as dark as dusk. It's far off, but not so far that I cannot hear the howls of the wind and the screams of the dead from my home."

The crowd gasps, but no one dares speak in the event they miss anything.

"The minor God no longer hibernates, but I know nothing of the cause."

"I can take a damn accurate guess." A burly fellow by the name of Dram separates from the crowd and approaches with an arrogant swagger. His long hair is reminiscent of candle flame, the matching facial hair draping his face in fire.

"Explain, Dram. What *do* you know?" My shoulders grow tense as I fold my arms over my chest, everyone knows he lusts for dramatics. Catching my tone, his face contorts from mindless arrogance to a threatening glare.

"There was a witch in our midst yesterday. She did something to us in the pub the other night, can't figure out what, but I'd bet my gram's left tit she's gettin' her karma with the giant out there."

A few of his fellow pub patrons nod in quiet agreement behind him.

"What lovely imagery. Thank you for that." The Jarl drawls, rolling his eyes and already turning away from him. Before Dram can open his mouth, he cuts him off, "Dram, as always you speak with a seedling of truth and an abundance of embellishment. I'm aware of two young women who traveled through our home just yesterday, but the only *witch* nearby is the Vala." The Jarl takes a moment of silence as his eyes skip around the crowd, surveying his people. "One does not simply have magic, and your confusion does not warrant such an accusation or all of us risk being witches in your eyes."

Even as the ominous danger looms overhead, much of the crowd snickers at Dram's public humiliation. He retreats through the crowd with his tail tucked and steam practically shooting from his ears in rage. As much as I love seeing the overgrown child that he is so humbled, it's time to acquire some answers with substance.

An intense beating of wings circle the sky where two black ravens descend upon us. One soars so closely to the crowd that they all have to duck to avoid it, while the other perches atop the pommel of my horse's saddle, looking directly at me.

The bird stares into my eyes, its own being too human like to mark this as a regular raven. The creature seems oddly sentient, and I'm convinced it's trying to keep my attention for a reason. The other raven caws from the sky, and only then does the one close to me look away. Freedom from the stare is short lived as it garners my attention by flicking its head to the side before flying off.

Does it want me to follow it?

"These bloody fucking birds! Somebody get me an arrow," an older man yells in frustration.

Apparently these two have been causing a bit of trouble in town as my curiosity to an earlier complaint of birds is answered.

"Hush your qualms, sir! There are urgent matters at hand. Surely you can handle two ravens once it's settled." The authority in my tone warrants no room for defiance, and the entire village silences once more.

I want this spectacle over with so I can find the birds again.

"Who amongst us has gone hunting in The Frostreik before?" A young man and his grandfather step forward, pride in their bravery evident in their puffed chests.

"We go every year, sir. We search for rare game not typical for our forests, usually to no avail," the young man declares. His elder gives a curt nod in confirmation.

"While hunting do you ever experience odd weather?" I ask curiously.

"Nothing more than the eternal snow and unnatural freezing temperatures of the land."

"Thank you for your help, sirs. Jarl, a word?"

He follows in stride as we disengage from the crowd into an empty stall in the nearby stables. I'm sure this is where the raven's head tilted. Once alone, he releases an exaggerated stream of air and runs his hand through his straight brown hair.

"Appreciate your help, Zander. The way you handle them is a testament to your days in my position." He claps a calloused hand on my shoulder, translating his admiration from words to gesture.

"It's the least I can do, Jarl. My decision to step down was sudden yet necessary, I'll always help when I can."

He shoots me a smirk that never even makes it close to his eyes, and lowers his gaze to a random spot on the straw bound floor.

"I hate to even speak the thought, but do you reckon this requires a message to...him?" His words are barely a whisper, too afraid to even say his name.

My lips part to speak until we are interrupted by the ravens, rushing into the adjacent stall and freezing us both with their menacing glares.

"What is this madness? Why are these creatures behaving in such a way?" The Jarl bustles toward the birds in an effort to shoo them away, yet they simply lower their gaze to meet his eyes, moving as one, the intensity causing him to pause. As soon as they are satisfied that he won't get closer to them, they both look back at me. I was correct before, these are clearly not typical ravens, I'd be wise to not to treat them as such.

Unable to make eye contact with both birds at once, I choose to reciprocate the gaze of the one closer to me. Its eyes appear to liquify, black tears pour down its feathers and onto the wooden gate on which it stands. It pulls me into a trance, unable to break free—desiring to stay.

Harbor trust in him no more,
Usurpers thrive in tattered gore.
His goal will be the end of all,
Do not be one to bow and fall.
Danger stalks both stone and ice,
The key must reach substantial heights.
We guide the hope of land once lost,
So hurry home to save thee crossed.

They wait where they are perched as I process their rhyme, aware of the Jarl's slackened jaw–he must have heard them as well. I haven't completely deciphered their meaning, but I acknowledge the impatient tension filling the small area where we stand.

"Jarl, I must return to Asa. Gather the lakelanders and distract them, let no one wander." I rush to leave the stalls, regret sinking my chest as I leave my friend confused in my wake.

"Zander, what in the Nine Realms is going on. Answer me this, then be on your way." Power dominates his voice, forcing me to stop in my tracks.

"The ravens know the reason for the storm. I do not yet know the extent of their riddle, but I do know what the Vala told my wife and I."

My breaths come heavier as adrenaline pumps through me; my life's greatest purpose is coming to fruition. His thick eyebrows are furled in confusion while his ice blue eyes bore into me with impatience and a desire for answers.

Doing my best to take a deep breath, I steady myself and recite the words told to us by the witch in the woods. "Asa and I must help the women in the snow. The first one grieves while the other still grows..." I falter as the next part does not come as clear to me after so much time. "The other still grows...a formidable foe lingers not far, royalty versus the Jotungangr." I imagine the giant undead monster in the snow at the mention of its name.

"Royalty? It could not mean..."

The sound of an entire forest of trees snapping to splinters courses through the air, shaking the ground beneath our feet. We both fall to the ground while black feathers, that are surely made from the night sky itself, span on either side of the ravens to keep their balance. Before either of us can say a word or attempt to stand, we are driven further to the ground with a horrifying rattled screech that permeates the air. Covering my ears does nothing to stop the sound from tearing apart my mind from the inside.

After what feels like minutes rather than seconds later, the scream of the undead comes to an end. Without hesitation, the ravens disappear into the shadows and I run home as quickly as my aging legs can carry me, trusting that the Jarl will do as I asked so the queens will be safe.

TWENTY-TWO

BREE

"Come on, love. You're doing amazing." His hand wipes the sweat that drips down my face, a gesture of comfort that only makes the heat radiating off my skin more intense. I force myself to breathe, only managing quick, sharp breaths.

"Get...her...out...NOW!" Exhaustion rattles my words, even my voice is begging for a break.

"She isn't positioned correctly, just give her a little more time to adjust herself befo–"

"*I SWEAR TO YOU, IF YOU MAKE ME DO THIS FOR ANOTHER SECOND YOU WILL REGRET EVER STEPPING ONTO THIS GODS FORSAKEN ISLAND!*" Amidst my pain and tears I make a mental note to apologize to my dear friend when this is all over.

"Signy, is it safe to attempt the other way?" He tries to speak quietly, although why he thinks I cannot hear him when he is still touching my face is beyond my comprehension.

She looks warily between my husband and I, contemplating the risks.

"Technically, I can try it now. You'll need to help her stay incredibly still, the slightest movement can have serious repercussions."

"I hold you both so very close to my heart, but if you do not get this child out of me in the next five minutes I will bring this entire building down to nothing but rubble. I have waited thirty excruciating hours to *meet my baby, who apparently is just as stubborn as her father. I can stay as still as death."*

"That is the nicest she'll be for the rest of the night, let's do this before she murders us both." Signy responds with an awkward chuckle as she gathers her equipment and behind rubbing a numbing ointment across my lower abdomen.

"I need you to take a few deep breaths, okay?"

I do as she asks and nod as I inhale as deeply as I'm able, my body testing my abilities with one of the strongest cramps thus far. As I exhale, I gradually lose feeling of everything below my breasts.

"It is incredibly important that there is no movement, do you understand?"

My husband and I nod in understanding and he moves his hand from my forehead to gently grasp my wrist. He has attempted to hold my hand once already and I nearly broke it. I can tell the moment she begins the first incision, working slowly to be as precise as possible. Once she's completed with the first cut, she'll begin a race against time to ensure my baby and I both survive.

Destrin turns his gaze from the procedure to watch me instead. He tries giving me a reassuring look, but can only manage a grimace—his fears are more powerful than his acting. To distract myself from what is happening to my lower half, I allow our hands to touch and try to assure him that everything will be okay. The gleam in his eyes relays his gratitude, but it's still not enough to put his worries to rest.

Minutes go by where we just look into each other's eyes, willing one another not to be afraid while also preparing our possible goodbyes. This type of procedure has not yet been successful in keeping both mother and child alive, but I like to think of myself as somewhat of a special case. We've done everything possible in order to guarantee my survival, no one could be more prepared to live through this than me.

At long last, a piercing wail graces my ears and my daughter is here, alive, and breathing. Her father stands as he takes her from Signy, who wrapped her in a traditional birth blanket before handing her over. As he sits back beside me, my friend gets to work closing me up. This is the part we've been dreading, but I've already made it further than most.

He scoots his chair as close to me as he can, leaning over my chest so he can gently place our daughter against my skin, holding her in place so I don't have to move my arms. Her cries were short-lived as she's already resting peacefully against me. I don't attempt to stop the tears from escaping, how could one not cry when they are looking at their soul personified?

It's not until Signy is on my other side, smiling down at us, that I realize she has finished. She finished, and we are both alive. A sob racks my chest and I grab her hand, squeezing it tightly in thanks and love.

"You are a master, Signy. Thank you, thank you for giving me this moment with her."

She pushes the hair stuck to my face behind my ear and gently places a kiss upon my cheek. She gives my husband a strong squeeze on his shoulder, and he kisses her hand in appreciation before she leaves the room, allowing us to look down at our little one.

"She's as beautiful as her mother. A feat I never thought possible."

"I can't believe how perfect she is, Des. Never did I think that I could love something like this, with such intensity." *Nothing can make me take my eyes off of her tiny nose and lips. I slowly trace my finger down the side of her face, her skin the softest I've ever felt. There has never been a feeling of such perfection as when she lies on my chest, sleeping peacefully in my arms.*

"Oh, sweet Annie. Of all the things I've ever held, the best by far is you."

"Bree."

"Shhh, just let me look at her a little longer, Des."
"Annie needs you, Bree. Wake up."
"Wake up?"

"Rise and shine, favorite Ragna of mine."

My eyes shoot open at the second voice, bringing me back from the safety of my dreams. Taking in the scene around me, I quickly realize I'm upside down, my ankles held to the ceiling with ice. My pulse is pounding through my head, and based on the extent of the throbbing, I'm guessing that I've been hanging here for much too long.

My eyes feel like they're going to be pushed out of my head any second, and using them requires too much effort. Trying to gather my complete surroundings proves to be pointless. I can only assume I'm still within The Frostreik. The cave appears to be made of ice-allowing a glacial blue glow in from the sunlight beyond. The last thing I remember is Annie falling while we ran from the– "Annie?"

"Annie!" Any desire for silence is tossed aside as my voice echoes through the cave. I need to find my daughter.

As soon as I try lifting my head, I regret it. Sharp pain shoots behind my eyes and darkness surrounds my vision, threatening to take the sense altogether. There will be no hope of helping her if I die because all of my blood is pooled in my head.

Choosing the lesser of two evils, I risk a miniscule movement of scanning the cave and spot our belongings in a pile against the opposite wall. The only sound is quiet breathing coming from behind me, and I pray to the Gods it's Annie.

I close my eyes in order to relieve some of the pressure, and focus on melting the ice that binds me. Within seconds my ankles are almost free and I push my magic a bit further to help me brace my fall to the glass-like floor. The impact was fine—silent, even—but my head pounds relentlessly now that I am horizontal. I lift myself up with ice jutting from the cave. The wall keeps my body upright while my head readjusts, making the room spin around me.

I can't afford the time needed to fully recover; I need to locate Annie. Following the direction I heard the breathing, I'm brought behind a jagged shard of broken ice, easily twice my height. My daughter hangs from her ankles as well, her face beet red, and her breathing labored. Lifting her upper body slowly, I rest her head on my shoulder while I work my magic the same as before, watching the shackles of ice melt. As soon as I have her down, I lean her against the ice wall, sitting beside her, allowing myself to regain my bearings. Annie remains unconscious, but at least she's breathing—that's what matters most.

My body begins to fade, demanding rest now that the immediate risk to our lives has been postponed. Although we're clearly in the home of something utterly terrifying, I cannot sense it nearby, allowing myself to close my eyes and let the darkness take me.

An incessant shaking pulls me from sleep, demanding I open my eyes and find the source. Through the haze of exhaustion, I see the outline of a man crouching before me, and another by Annie. As the seconds pass, the details of their faces become increasingly clear and familiar. They both wear dark, fur-lined cloaks with tall, leather boots that reach their knees. Their black hair windswept and crystal eyes practically glowing with the frost around us. Their voices are a relief to my ears–promising safety and hope.

"Awake, sweet Bree, we've come to help." One man begins.

"Healing is needed from damage dealt." His brother finishes.

Elvind reaches a soft hand forward to help me stand. Once on my feet, I trap him in a crushing embrace—grateful for their help, yet again. His arms wrap around my shoulders and he reciprocates the hug tenfold. His scent is nostalgic, but I can't put my finger on where I've smelled it before.

Aeven is still crouched before Annie, attempting to rouse her from her comatose state. I peek around Elvind's arm, Aeven furrowing his brow as he inspects her, contemplating the reason for her continued sleep. Worry anew spreads through my chest, she may be alive but something bars her from consciousness.

"Can you help her?" I barely recognize my voice, resembling a fearful child too scared to speak.

His fluorite gaze meets mine and he gives a reassuring smirk. "Of course we can, that is our task."

I wait for the typical rhyme in response from Elvind, but he stays silent, looking down at me with a blank smile when I glance at him expectantly. Perceiving my confusion, they simply look at each other and snicker—clearly finding something humorous between them. So evidently, they enjoy toying with me as much as assisting me—I'll keep that in mind.

Aeven lifts Annie effortlessly into his arms, while Elvind keeps one arm around my shoulder as they walk us out together. Once we reach the mouth of the cave, I realize there are no horses, carriages, or anything of the sort, completely forgetting that most animals cannot reach this far into The Frostreik due to the high snow. I assume the boys arrived here in their raven forms, but how do they expect to get us out quickly enough to not be captured, or killed, by whatever is out here again?

"How are we–"

Aeven cuts me off with a sharp noise, signaling me to be quiet. He wears a look of determination while meeting eyes with his brother, speaking some silent language amongst each other. I haven't known them for long, but they've never worn such serious masks as this in my presence before.

At long last, Elvind whispers their plan. "One at a time, or nothing at all. Hide in the dark, or risk a fine maul. Something you seek awaits just below, blood of the Father grants passage to flow."

I memorize his words, another riddle to solve. There is one thing that is clear in the meaning; they will take Annie to safety while I am left behind to find what I came here for—Gungnir.

The spear is the entire reason we've come in this direction in the first place, aside from keeping away from heavier civilization. I nod to them both, understanding my task.

Satisfied that I'm confident in my next steps, Aeven lays Annie back in the snow and wraps his cloak around her. The two turn back into their sleek bird forms in a cloud of star sprinkled shadow, take opposite ends of the cloak in their beaks, and lift Annie into the air with them—their strength further proof of their mysterious magic. Before sending off, I am graced with one more warning:

Beware of the dead when you take what they guard,
You've seen them before, rotting and scarred.
The test of the blood will fall upon thee,
He only allows the presence of three.
We will return, our dearest Bree.
Do not fret, do not leave.
But most important of all,
Do not die, and do not freeze.

BEST BY FAR

After a finger-numbing amount of time searching for some sort of clue, dragging my hands across the icy walls of the cave, I finally notice a peculiar crack along a wall that doesn't glow as brightly as the others. At first I was shocked by the faint glowing that shines out of every imperfection in the ice, so when I walked by this particular crack before, I figured it just wasn't being touched by sunlight from the outside. It could be covered in a deep layer of snow to explain the lack of glow, but upon second glance, the crack of ice has a minuscule pull beneath it that I hadn't felt before—ancient magic. Magic this old has a different weight than what I wield. It is much stronger than my own, more *pure*.

The closer I step, the more certain of the ancient presence I become. It's almost undetectable, easy to miss in my urgency to find something more obvious before. The power pouring through even smells old, like the pages of a dusty book. It sings to the magic in my bones, like an ancestor to my powers.

The darkness behind the ice sends shivers down my body, there's a presence within that urges me closer, and I'm unable to determine its intentions. Alas, the intentions mean nothing if I cannot reach whatever is within anyway. I recite Elvind's riddle quietly to myself, finding it is easier to think through a puzzle if I talk my way through it. "Blood of the Father grants passage to flow."

Odin is known as the Allfather, the creator of us all. Seeing as the weapon below belongs to him, it would make sense that he would have warded the chamber with a blood ritual. How is one expected to find his blood? It sounds like an impossible task, and I remember the words that I spoke to Annie about a lifetime ago. *"We are meant to be on that throne and the Gods will allow us to do impossible things in order to reclaim it."*

So the Allfather is testing me then.

The test of blood will fall upon thee,
He only allows the presence of three.

The boys already told me this, I knew this was a test. Short of finding the God himself, the only other way to obtain the Odin's blood is through his direct bloodline—which brings me to the presence of three. Does this mean three mortals on this plane have Odin's blood flowing through their veins? What an honor that would be. My family magic comes in part from him, I can only imagine having his blood as well.

So where do I begin my search for one of these three? I must assume they are his children, the stories tell nothing of siblings, or even parents for that matter. He has sired some of the Gods, like Thor, but they would not linger here nor have use for his spear. There is also the expectation from my feathery friends that I can finish this task before they return for me—which would mean...could Pa be right?

I pull a dagger from my small pack, and push the tip against the palm of my hand. Uncertainty clenches my heart, my lungs can barely take full breaths, and both my hands shake—unwilling to puncture the skin. Pa has never backed down from his theory of my mystery lineage—that of my father. I've never taken it too seriously. Pa simply just wants the best for me, and proof that I'm more than just another heir to the throne. I think of how my family has always commented on the strength of my abilities. Pa would imply it had something to do with magic being from both of my parents.

Seeing as the Regent, who is the only other we know of with magic, cannot be my sire, that would leave us to believe that a God may have paid a visit to us mortals. What are the chances of that? The Gods are not to interfere with the fates woven by the Norns, but the odds of a God happening upon my mother, the heir to Asvalda, is too much to handle.

The further I go down this path of thought, the heavier my chest grows. The implications are too heavy for a journey already so complicated. How much should be put on a mortal's shoulders? Being heir to a throne isn't enough, so making sure their sires are both magical beings should be added on as well? Who else has magic besides my family and the Regent? These questions are driving me mad.

But he's not the only one with magic, is he? The two carrying my daughter to safety at this moment have an entirely new kind of magic to me, not dark like the Regent, nor as simple like my own, but somewhere between. I shake my head in an attempt to scatter the thoughts. I can contemplate this later. For now, I need to see if my blood is the answer, and process what that means later on—when I can question the ravens as well.

I close my eyes to ground myself, and with a shaky breath, I drive the knife into my palm. The tip of the blade goes deep enough for a small pool of blood to form in the curve of my hand. I watch the wall of ice in front of me as I place my hand against the hairline crevice, waiting for something to happen—anxious that nothing will.

A faint tingling sensation brushes across my palm, and when I rip my hand back to my chest, I watch as my blood is absorbed into the ice, all the way to the other side. The thought to wrap my wound takes priority, until I notice that the pain in my hand has disappeared. Expecting to see a short gash with a smear of dark red, I'm shocked when there is nothing.

The ancient magic was thirsty for every drop it seems, and healed me in the process. A sudden popping noise fills the cave, the ice in front of me splitting and cracking further until there is a tight opening large enough to squeeze myself through. A chill runs through me, deeper than just the surrounding temperature. The darkness beckons me forward, into the depths of nothingness.

Entering a blackened tunnel with a sentient presence within is never a smart idea, especially when said tunnel hides inside a cave where an undead giant resides. I wedge myself through, my chest flattened against the ice, forcing the chill deeper than my bones and into my very soul. A gasp escapes me as my entire body is held firmly by the ancient cold that desecrates the tunnel. It's not a numbing sensation, thank the Gods, but it's not pleasant in the slightest. There's one thing that comes to mind as I quickly become convinced I'll never feel warmth again, and that is death.

Stone steps descend further underground, wide enough for me to get my bearings as I put one foot before the other blindly. I walk for what feels like hours—and maybe I have. It's so hard to tell when my body already aches and I'm amid the absence of any light, landmark, or knowledge of what awaits me.

Echoes narrate each of my steps and as soon as I wonder how far down this could possibly go, torches on either side of the tunnel ignite in tandem. Amber light spreads ahead of me and yet, the flames are unable to penetrate the aching cold, and there's still no end in sight. I'm able to descend at a brisk pace with less fear of falling, and stumble upon a sudden landing—where was this a moment ago?

With a shadow surrounding my sight, I can only see directly ahead of me, and I realize rather quickly that I'm no longer alone in the tunnel. A small animal brushes its cushioned fur against my leg, jumping in front of me. It makes eye contact with me, beckoning for me to follow, except—I know this animal, and it is not Mead.

Beauty.

What is Nan's familiar doing here? She disappeared with Nan's last breath, this shouldn't be possible. Beauty nips at my shoe, the small hazelnut rabbit impatient with me. I brace myself with my hands on either side of the tunnel to keep myself upright, the shadows beginning to make my head spin. I decide to follow the rabbit, if some part of Nan is here, guiding me, then I need to follow.

She rushes through the tunnel, keeping pace with me. We pass hundreds of openings to other paths as we run, and I realize that without my guide, I may have been lost to this darkness forever. My vision is limited here, but Beauty knows the way. My steps echo ahead of us, and occasionally, a subtle dripping from the ceiling synchronizes with the echoes—should it be warm enough for any of the ice to melt?

My unvoiced question is answered when there's a faded light far ahead. It's a gentle glow that forces me to move faster.

Beauty stops to face me, and I trip over myself to avoid toppling her. I brace myself on the wet, stone wall beside me and find the part of Nan's soul sitting beside me. Her usual amber eyes are now bright green, the color of fresh grass in the Spring—Nan's eyes. She turns her head to look down the tunnel at the small, mysterious glow before catching my gaze again. With a quick nod, she dashes so far ahead that I lose track of her.

The world seems to shift as the pain I felt before goes away entirely, leaving me in Odin's tunnel, no Beauty in sight.

TWENTY-THREE

ANNIE

Consciousness attempts to pull me forward, my eyes yearn to open and assess the situation, and yet, I can't bring myself to care. There is such warmth embracing my body, as though I have been dipped inside of a tub filled with steaming water, and it's glorious.

The floral scent of lavender swirls around me, whispering to my aching muscles to relax—do not move, do not wake. There is a persistent ringing in my ears, intent on ruining the most calming bath I've ever experienced. The more I focus on it, the louder it gets, until it's all that I can hear. The airy swirls of lavender and scalding water can no longer win the fight to subdue my consciousness, and I'm finally forced to open my eyes.

I'm surrounded by steam, the floral scent coming from the bundles of lavender that hang from each corner of the small room. Small circle windows decorate each wall, almost touching the ceiling, and too high for anyone to take a peek through from outside.

Realizing that I *am* bathing in scalding water, I panic, imagining some stranger stripping me of my clothes without my consent. The water splashes over the edges of the wooden tub as I sit straight up, checking my body to find any evidence of abuse, only to find that I am still wearing the long black undershirt that I always have on under my clothes.

A muffled voice calls through the door across from me and I recognize it immediately. "Little Ragna, little Ragna, do finish up. Your mother awaits and fights the corrupt."

Fights the corrupt?

"Speak plainly for once in your life, raven." I spit at them.

"Oh sweet Ann, did you hit your head? Surely you remember the great undead!"

Of course I remember the *great undead*. If I never saw an undead snow giant again, it would still be too soon.

"Wait, where is my mother?" I step out of the tub slowly, sore from our tragic failure through the Frostreik, and find a pile of clean rags folded on a stool to dry myself with next to fresh clothing that I put on. When I open the door I'm met with crystal gazes, folded arms, and messy black hair. I'm shocked to see the ravens in their human forms; they look to be the same age as myself. I shake my head to recover from the surprise of seeing them like this and demand answers. "Where am I? And where is she? Speak without rhymes, if she needs my help then you must be quick with your words."

"A pleasure milady, I am Aeven. Lakewood nears, so do the craven."

"Elvind here, but worry not. The helpful man provides a cot."

With a deep sigh and defeated eye roll, I patiently wait for an explanation from one of the two. At some point they need to tell me what is going on without the dramatics, and clearly my mother can't be in imminent danger if they are standing here guarding a bathhouse with their riddles. After a long, tension coated silence, Elvind obliges.

"You were hurt but your mother was there.
She kept you safe in the vivid nightmare.
While distracted was he, the Jotungangr.
We took flight with you wrapped
In a cloak protected from anger.

She stays behind on a hunt for the truth,

And with it will find a spear of much use."

He ends his tale in a whisper, leaving my mind reeling. So the elusive snow monster, Jotungangr, that haunts the stories of Lakewood is indeed protecting Gungnir.

"What truth is she to find? How will she get back to us?" I wonder how she will know where to find us at the same moment I realize that I don't know where I am either.

Aeven wraps a warm arm around my shoulders and begins leading me towards a small cabin just ahead. The air has an unnerving chill to it, like it will not be satisfied until it reaches deep inside my bones. Dried leaves crunch beneath our feet, the frigid soil beneath working with the air to freeze me through my bare feet. Large billows of smoke rise from the cabin's chimney, promising an escape from the cold that wishes to poison me, I'm sure.

Just before we can open the cabin door, Aeven stops me in our tracks, turning me by my shoulders to face him. His fluorite irises hypnotize me, they allow me to focus on nothing but this protector holding me.

"Listen, dear Annie, you are safe here. Your mother is strong but her way is not clear. We must be off. We will bring her back. We can only hope the spear won't fight back."

He presses his forehead to mine in a gesture of promise. He wishes to assure me that they'll do everything they can to return her to me, for it is clear how important she is to them as well.

"Aeven, who are you to us?" I feel Elvind step closer, he places a hand on his brother's shoulder, matching his hypnotic gaze with his own aquamarine eyes. When he speaks, all fear leaves my body. Why do I find myself trusting these men so explicitly?

"Our truth is our own, but we promise you this, we'll do all that we can to protect you from his."

And with that, they are ravens once more, flying towards the tormented sky where they left my mother.

TWENTY-FOUR
BREE

This is it.

The stories hold nothing to the actual magnificence of Gungnir. I'm almost too scared to touch the spear as it lies upon a slate of obsidian, runes along the shaft glow a striking blue, illuminating the large cavern I've found myself in.

I can feel a pull to the spear, but a warning as well. This has all been too simple, despite being attacked. I'm blissfully aware that not just anyone would have been able to open the secret tunnel, a discovery that I'm not quite ready to process. Even then, there must be something else, I cannot just take the spear and leave. Odin would not protect this so inattentively.

Beware of the dead when you take what they guard,
You've seen them before, rotting and scarred.

The words of the ravens echo in my mind, and I immediately still. It's an odd sensation, feeling all of the color leach from my face as the blood hides deep within me—feeling the fear that I do. I haven't come across another creature like the ones who attacked my village—killing my husband. What a cruel twist of fate that they're what I will be forced to face the moment I take the spear from its bed of obsidian.

The Allfather...*my* father...tests me with such torment.

It has been weeks since I have handled such a weapon, and never one so powerful. I try to prepare myself with a deep, shaky breath, my hand hovering over the rune-carved shaft, and I take it.

I half expected chaos to ensue the moment the spear was in my hand, and yet nothing happens—no echo within the spherical cavern, and nothing changes.

Besides Gungnir itself.

The glow that moments ago defended me from the dark sputters out in my hand, stealing my sight and any courage I may have tricked myself into having. I retreat to the slab of stone, needing something at my back so that I can protect my front.

Knowing what is coming, yet not knowing when, is a cruel torture. I push my magic away from me, trying to feel anything that may be hiding in the shadows. Yet there's nothing. The only thing that has changed has been the lighting. Could the boys have been mistaken? Could the dead have been the giant we have already faced and I will be forced to escape it once again?

My leg muscles twitch slightly, reading myself to move, until I hear it. A rattling breath that haunts the darkness, a sword dragging across stone slices through the silence, and the rancid stench of death consumes the entire space. I can hear them moving closer, so I push my magic away from me once more, hoping to sense them in the absence of sight.

Draugr surround me entirely.

There's a small gap between myself and the first draugr that advances on me. If we both raised our arms toward the other, my hand would be trapped in the decaying prison of his skeletal body. Realizing the undead man is so close to me already sets my mind into a panic. Any essence of past training flees my mind, leaving me frozen in fear—*again*. Flashes of my village burning invade my eyes. Villagers screaming, men fighting, Destrin dying, Annie crying over his body.

Thinking of my family forces the spear to rise in my hands as I pierce the air in front of me, knowing I aim directly for its throat. There's a gurgling moan too close to me, and the sludge that runs through its veins splash onto my hands as I force the spear to the right, severing its head completely.

With a nauseating thud, the body collapses to the ground and more scuffling feet approach. The dead here seem to be moving much slower than those that came to Gledibyr, not nearly as quick with their attack but still horrifying.

I can't keep forcing waves of magic out to find them, it will run me dry. The longer I take to decide what to do, the more frantic my breathing becomes. The rattles that come from their rotted throats, the cracking of their bones as they stalk toward me, it is all too much.

I'm losing control of my breathing, my head feels too heavy for my body and causes me to drop to the floor, Gungnir tight in my grip.

Once more, just one more push.

I'll find the exit to the tunnel and run, surely they cannot keep up when they have taken this long to get to me already. I close my eyes, praying to Gods that somehow they'll disappear and this will just be a horrible vision, a nightmare that plagues me like any other night.

Pushing aside my prayers, I focus on where the next draugr stands. My magic feels nothing immediately surrounding me. That can't be right, they move rather slow but not *that* slow. I can't sense any of them anywhere, even though moments ago it sounded like at least ten of them were inching toward me. No clatter of disintegrating metal reverberates through the air, or the sick noises of their movements. In fact, there are no sounds at all. Just silence. Not the silence of an open field, nor the silence of a monastery. Not even the silence that I just experienced before grabbing Gungnir.

This silence accompanies the essence of nothing. There is no such thing as sound in this space. Someone has not just covered my ears, they have taken the very existence of sound completely. My only natural sense available to me in this test plucked from my very ears.

So, I open my eyes.

Scattered along the room are small, glowing orbs. There is no movement amongst them, no rhyme or reason in the way they are placed. They don't emulate the same glow as the runes did, as they are not meant to guide me *through* the darkness.

They are meant to drag me *into* it.

I gather any semblance of self preservation left and quickly stand, spear ready to pierce through any that come too near. I can't hear my feet against the stone or the fearful shake of each breath as I begin to turn, intending to track every set of dead, glowing white eyes that watch me. I'm careful not to allow any of them out of my sight as my eyes skate across the room, blurring from being strained in such darkness.

The anticipation of when they will attack at any second pushes my chest into itself, threatening to crush my lungs. The tension in my body is so strong that everything hurts as I stand ready. This is what they do, they stand in silence like they are waiting for a signal to riot.

Destrin flashes before me, illuminated by fire, waiting for the draugr to attack, to do anything at all. *Move Destrin.*

I try to scream. Do not wait for them. *Attack, and kill them before they kill you.*

He can't hear me, but he senses me. With sword in hand and body ready for battle, he looks away from the threat to reach my gaze.

Don't look at me you fool, look ahead!

No matter what I scream, nothing can be heard and his brow furrows—worried for me. Sobs assault my chest, tears race down my cheeks, my throat burns from soundless screams, knowing what is to come.

The entire scene changes before me. I'm no longer in my burning village watching my husband die for the thousandth time. Instead, he stands in front of me, one hand cupping my face and the other resting on my hip. We stand in a frozen field of snow, nothing around for miles besides the tundra.

Molten chocolate irises stare back at me, a color I haven't been able to picture for years. I can't help myself, I drop the spear and hold my love's face in my hands, warm beneath my touch. I'm completely enraptured by him; I cannot even remember how I got here, where I really am. My tears run slower, fueled by love rather than terror. I need his lips on mine, to feel his kiss once more.

I long for it—for him.

Before I can be rid of the distance between us, he opens his mouth slightly, as if to say something. His hands fall to his sides but he doesn't move away. His eyes no longer pull me in from the desire to have him again, they pull me in by magic–forcing me to look at him. Being unable to move has never sat right with me, it has always induced panic immediately—this is no different even while looking into my dead husband's eyes. Frozen still, unable to scream, unable to look away, I watch Destrin decompose before me.

His chocolate gaze spoils as a milky white cloud takes over. His full, olive toned cheeks sink into the hollow of his mouth. His thinning skin turns gray and grows tight across his cheekbones and jaw. The once luscious black hair flowing to his shoulders loses all moisture, shrinking to half of its length as each strand dries until it's straw. Beetles and maggots thrive in his beard, feasting on the fast rotting flesh just beneath. The black sludge of *their* blood oozes from *his* nose, trickling slowly down into his open mouth.

I have dreamt of my husband's death almost every night for thirteen years. Sometimes he's killed in the woods where we met, other times I watch him fight valiantly against the undead until he is slain. But I've never watched him become the creature that killed him.

Nothing within me moves besides my rapidly beating heart that urges my body to leave, run, survive. His transformation is complete, no longer can I recognize the man with a boisterous laugh and seductive one-liners. Before me stands the physical manifestation of what I have condemned my soulmate to in death.

His jaw suddenly detaches from his face altogether, hanging unnaturally on one side, barely holding on. A fiery scene from Gledibyr of a draugr's jaw snapping off in front of Destrin flashes in my eyes before coming back to his own jaw hanging. His empty white eyes beckon my attention as they slowly acquire a faint glow. A high pitched scream rips from his gaping maw, shattering my ear drums and influencing a scream of my own—one that I can now hear.

So distracted by the pain in my ears, the ringing in my head and the scream of demons, I completely miss the quick movement made by Des—the draugr. My voice is cut short, replaced by wet choking. My chest does not rise with any breath. There's too much pressure, something pushing against me that won't allow me to get any air.

I'm brought back to Destrin lying on the ground beneath me, spear lodged inside of him, taking his life away. I mourn for my husband. I mourn for my fatherless daughter, and I fear the creatures that took him from me. I wipe the tears from my eyes to get a better look at him, to memorize his face one last time—but it is not my love that lies beneath me any longer.

It's me.

TWENTY-FIVE
RAVENS

Ice & Snow,
Frost from below,
The father wanders near.

He tests the weak,
Lest they be reaped,
He hides his secrets here.

Jotungangr hunts the field,
It guards the secret here to wield.
The only ones to go below,
Must hide their fear and travel slow.

They bleed the blood,
The blood of mine,
And down they go to deathly grime.

Can they make it?
Can they take it?
Take the secret hidden here?

Two fly fast,

BEST BY FAR

In barrens, vast.
An open sea,
Most cannot flee.
A tunnel glows,
So down they go,
To save their sister, free.

Flames erupt from cones of bone,
To light the cavern death calls home.

The dead rise up,
They plan to sup,
Feasting them back to stone.

A princess cries,
Dread in her eyes,
She sees such horror there.

She thinks of him,
The night he died,
Spears cut through the air.

In her chest,
It chose to rest,
It cannot be...
She failed the test.

This cannot be,
The Vala sees,
A future with her there.

A brother friend lands next to her,
A sight he does so ponder.

The draugr hoard,
With rusty swords,
surround her body yonder.

He pecks her leg,
She swats at thee.
The movement weak
Lost in fantasy.

A beak doth pinch,
The sallow skin.
She must awake,
Unite with kin.

Another assault,
As quick as the first.
Her eyes open wide,
Noticing a curse.

Runes only glow
With the magic of Gods,
Her chest is alight
She brandishes claws.

With unconscious power,
She sets them aflame.

They fall in great heaps,
Their magic in shame.

Meeting black beads,
With eyes made of hazel,
Her smile glows brighter
With loving appraisal.

The clouds fog her mind,
It needs a great rest.
This magic of his,
Was a treacherous test.

Visions will plague her,
Like they already have.
Her fear will evade her,
As time doth go past.

Carried quite freely,
In the chill of the sky,
Bree shivers slightly,
Spear by her side.

Blood that goes missing,
Wounds do no weeping,
Her chest rises slowly,
And falls just the same.

TWENTY-SIX
BREE

I've always been thankful that my nightmares never cursed me with a fear of the forest. While there are occasional images of the undead emerging from shadows of thick foliage, and a menacing man radiating evil that holds Mead captive, there are many memories that overshadow those fears with their light.

Destrin carried me through the woods to safety when we first met, rays of light shining through the leaves above to create a golden halo around his beautiful black hair. His eyes were molten amber in the sun and they sparkled with genuine good nature. I fell in love with those eyes and his aura the moment he cradled me in his arms and began teasing me before he even knew my name.

That is the forest I choose to remember. That is the glow of his eyes that I will *always* think of.

None of the darkness and torturous visions will ever tarnish or replace those memories in my heart, even if they continue to haunt my dreams.

Three days have passed since I found Gungnir, and every morning I make a point to sit in the grass outside of Asa and Zander's cabin while I drink my tea. Eventually the boys will join me, fluttering from one tree to another so that things don't remain too still. They worry for me after all of the mind games in Odin's Cavern, and I don't blame them. When the wind is too still and there are no signs of life, my vicious thoughts will take control, expecting something horrible to happen.

In the absence of noise, I fear the worst and my chest tightens as my nerves form into its treacherous little ball that rises into my throat, lodging itself there and making it difficult to breathe.

Aeven will toss himself around in the clouds while Elvind sings to the critters in the trees. It seems discovering that we share a Divine Father has encouraged them to be more attentive now that it is no longer a secret. Rather than solely appearing when danger is imminent, they have stayed by our sides the entire three days, ensuring that I'm not only physically well, but doing okay mentally as well.

When I bathe or retire to bed, they turn their attention to Annie. Sometimes I can hear Aeven getting her to laugh and Elvind will tell her all kinds of stories from the Gods. She worries for me too, and it wears her down not knowing how she can help. I appreciate that she has the boys to alleviate some of that weight from her shoulders.

The night they brought me here, Asa helped me bathe in their steam room. She washed my hair and soothed my mind with her calm tone and hanging lavender. Afterwards, they showed me to their family area. Two plush chairs were near the small fireplace, mounted animal heads from Zander's hunting trips lined the walls like trophies, and a very fluffy area rug decorated the wooden floor. They live a cozy life here, and their home is incredibly inviting and warm.

I was given one of the plush chairs and sank into it like I was drifting on a cloud. Asa took the other, facing me. Annie crossed her legs on the floor, leaning back against my chair to be near me, and the boys took their human forms and stood on either side of our host's seat. Zander stepped outside to begin prepping for dinner. We had sat in silence for quite a while. No one wanted to break that silence, but all wanted to know what had happened. Aeven and Elvind had seen what was happening both in my visions as well as reality, but were still curious about my survival.

"I can't take this anymore. Mother, what happened down there? How did you find it?" A war between curiosity and worry lace her words, the awe in her tone winning.

Thus began my tale of everything I had discovered. My blood is the blood of Odin—the God of Gods himself. It made me suspect that the two boys in front of me were his children as well, and it was proven when I witnessed them in Odin's Cavern with me, where only the three with his blood could enter. Annie was curious about their mother, but they're unaware of who she is, and seeing as they were raised by their steward, they cannot ask our father.

I told them of the glowing runes on Gungnir and how they sputtered into darkness as soon as I took hold of it. Shame took over as I described how badly the draugr scared me; nothing has ever made me freeze in fear the way I do when I am faced with those monstrosities. I have been trained vigorously to put aside any and all feelings when fighting, especially fear. After Destrin's death, I did everything I could think of to ensure that I would never freeze in front of them again, convincing myself that I would have no problem in the future. And yet, I proved weak. I described the visions the best I could muster, leaving out some of the details regarding Destrin's appearance so Annie doesn't have to imagine her father in such a way.

Lastly, I told them of the Gungnir in my chest. It punctured my lung just as Destrin's had been when he was slain. The ravens kept me conscious once they arrived, and just seeing them there, my brothers, fueled me with a sense of justice. With nothing but a thought, I brought every draugr to the ground in a fury of flames, and the runes began to glow once more. I pulled Gungnir from my chest with ease, leaving no wound behind, and it glowed brilliantly in my grasp, like it had been waiting for me. Exhaustion took over and I woke up with a blanket wrapped around me and a warm cloth on my head.

Asa's eyes were filled with amazement the entire time I spoke, she gasped in all the right places and teared up when I spoke of my husband. My brother's wore matching smirks as they listened to a story that needn't be told to them, and what I assumed to be pride glistened in their eyes while listening anyway. My daughter stayed uncharacteristically quiet the entire time, despite her eagerness for details. I feel badly that she worries herself with what I go through. I wish I could convince her that I am well; she needn't be weary of my mind.

Only the crackles and pops from the fire sound in the room; everyone is too deep in unraveling a piece of the mystery of Odin's Cavern to speak their theories. I have a few questions myself, but I wait to see what the others think before voicing them.

Asa clears her throat and places her hands in her lap one on top of the other before breaking the silence. "How were you able to kill all of the draugr at once? Have you done that before?"

My brow furrows and I focus on the thread that my hands have mindlessly pulled from my shirt. The former is something I wonder as well. "I can't even begin to grasp where that power came from. As soon as I saw the boys, I regained all of the strength the draugr leached from me before. I gained a sort of confidence, but I also knew that I couldn't let them be hurt or killed trying to protect me. I–I can't let that happen again." I turn my head toward the fire, unwilling to allow my mourning to take hold in this moment.

This time, Annie has the answers. "You have used that power before. Maybe not in that exact way, but you've done it nonetheless."

"What do you speak of, little one? I would remember using magic like that, it was more powerful than I've *ever* felt."

She readjusts so that she now faces the hearth; the flames making her auburn hair practically glow in the darkening cabin. Her eyes dart from her hands in her lap to my gaze, I can feel her nerves without even pushing my magic to her.

"Pa told me about it. The night that father was killed—you did it then." Guilt weighs her down, shoulders slumping over her crossed legs and chin practically touching her chest. She takes a moment before she continues, mimicking my habit of pulling at loose threads in clothing. "You and I...we didn't notice. We were holding his hands, saying goodbye. Your grief, it must have exploded from you. Pa said that they all fell when father died."

My head begins spinning, I have to grip the arms of the chair to steady myself. How could that have happened without my notice? I heard the swords of my neighbors continuing to fight afterwards...didn't I?

"I know what you're thinking. I remember hearing the swords behind us; I thought they were still fighting the draugr. I even mentioned that to Pa. He said that sound was them beheading the corpses in case they came back."

When Annie finally looks at me, I know what she must see looking back at her. Denial floods through my veins, a sort of betrayal bobbing through the onslaught of emotion. Blood drains from my face, leaving behind the forming beads of sweat on my freezing skin.

"Who...why..."

Annie saves me from trying to form a sentence. She takes my hands in hers as she kneels in front of me so close that her stomach is against my knees. "He said that all of Gledibyr knew who you were at that moment. Who *we* were. He spoke to them soon after—the entire village swore to secrecy. You haven't been awakened to your true power—even lineage—until now. He knew you weren't ready to learn what you were capable of yet." One of her hands lifts to my chin, refusing to let me descend when she knows I should rise.

The betrayal lessens in my heart, aware that Pa's decision was wise—as deceitful as it feels. A sense of wonder flowers in its place. Appreciation. *Love*. At my lowest point, in a loss of control transfigured into power, the people of Gledibyr were there for me—in a way I would have never known. Lost in a world where secrets are currency—where we are the prize—my village swore to protect us.

Zander's warm hand gently grips my shoulder, startling me. I hadn't even heard him enter the cabin. When I meet his hazel gaze, the deep lines of his face pull into a smile while his eyes crinkle in the corners, alight with adoration. "Bree, that is a true display of honor. Presented with a monumental secret such as your identity, your people had two options. On one hand, they could sell you out to the Regent in hopes of saving themselves and their family from his wrath. On the other, they could keep you and *your* family safe, fully aware of the risks. From the sound of it, they chose the latter without hesitation. To me, that shows the respect for a true leader—a true Queen."

I squeeze his hand in thanks, afraid to speak in case my words break with emotion. Despite my efforts, tears pool in my eyes—threatening to spill over any second. Where there was once a room full of confusion and worry, there now stands five loved ones, old and new, brimming with pride and determination.

"One last thing, before we rest; it seems our Bree passed one more test." Aeven saunters to my left side, hand held out for mine. Elvind follows his lead, practically gliding to my right in the same motion.

"It seems, I think, we all agree; the Ragna girls will soon be Queens."

I can't say I'm thrilled to be back near Lakewood after the not-so-warm welcome we received passing through previously. Luckily, Zander and Asa heard of our experience and decided to bring us to a trail close enough to hear the bustling of the small town, yet avoids the people completely.

The homely couple told our merry band of bandits about their past visit with a Vala over breakfast. Zander explained that this is how they knew they needed to be ready when the time came, though he lacked the knowledge of who it was that they would be helping. Annie, having never heard of a Vala, asked what we should expect.

"The Vala is a type of witch who lives in our neighboring forest. We go to their hut whenever we are unsure of our path, or if we need some guidance." Asa explains, walking arm-in-arm with Annie. They lean their heads in close together like they are sharing a secret between only them.

I'm grateful for their relationship. Having never met Tessa or Nan, Asa seems to be filling that grandmotherly void for Annie effortlessly. She dotes on Annie like she is her own, it warms my heart that Annie can experience a love like this, even only knowing each other for such a short time.

"Is it magic?" Annie asks in a hushed whisper.

"No, my dear," Asa responds, "It is something else entirely. Your mother was born of the Gods, but the Vala was made *by* them."

The walk to the Vala's hut was only a couple of hours by foot. When we suddenly stop at a small clearing of trees, I share a suspicious glance with my daughter. Before us is nothing but a large pile of dried leaves, with a thick blanket of snow, then more dried leaves and twigs sticking out at odd angles throughout the misshapen mound. Intending to inquire what kind of trickery Asa has attempted, I step in front of her—praying to the Gods I'm wrong.

"You *are* wrong, child. Get inside." The voice is hoarse yet loud. It sounds like autumn leaves being blown down a trail and the harrowing whistle of winter winds.

Spinning around, I'm shocked to see that the mound of leaves has grown exponentially. It looks as it did before, only now there is a thin entryway—a thick quilt to block the chilled breeze. The shadow of a humanoid figure peaks from the quilt, only bone white fingers visible as they peel back the makeshift door. "How did you hear me?" I ask.

"I didn't hear you," replies the thin, raspy voice, "I saw you. Get in, I will not say it again."

Asa pushes Annie and I forward, ushering us to enter the Vala's home without her. "We will just be outside, dears. There is nothing to fear, the Vala is here to help, not harm."

A pang of shame strikes me, aware I almost accused Asa of tricks. I take her hand and nod my thanks, walking forward with Annie following closely behind.

Thin veils of smoke hang in the air, and the smell of patchouli assaults my nose. The blanket of snow outside acts as insulation, resting on braided branches that form the structure of the mound—which is surprisingly larger from the inside. Small bones tied together with twine hang from the braids, all varying shapes and sizes. Most seem to be from animals, but there are a few questionable ones. There are few furnishings in the home; a pile of furs take up the back corner that is sectioned off with a thin woven sheet. The rest of the space has small wooden stools that host moss and webs scattered in what must be the sitting area.

My eyes quickly shift to a stack of furs and rags piled in such a way that they form a throne-like seat where the figure now sits. Long ago I learned that there are different types of Vala's. Some are merely women who can see glances into what will come, or even small prophecies—these are the völva. Others, like this one, are said to be ancient witches created by the Gods to help guide the humans in their everyday lives. They can see the future as well, but are known to be incredibly cryptic, and only choose to share bits and pieces they find relevant.

The Vala sits upon their throne of furs and gestures for us to be seated. Though I've heard about their abilities; I've never seen an Ancient Vala in person until now. Their face is void of eye sockets, skin flat against their face from their nose up. Sickly gray leather stretches across their bones, leaving no room for flesh in between. Despite the colder temperatures outdoors, the Vala is barely dressed, only donning a necklace of bones that hangs over a bare chest of jutting ribs, and the bottom half of an animal skin robe tied across their waist. Black wiry hair forms long dreadlocks down their shoulders and back, and their lips are dyed a similar color.

Once we are both seated, we wait patiently for the Vala to say something. Despite the lack of eyes, they *stare* into our very beings, searching for something within us for what feels like hours, until they finally speak. "Tell me the reason two of the heirs of Asvalda have come to my dwelling."

I swallow my shock, a vala's knowledge knows no bounds. "You once told a local couple how they would one day need to help two women. They have done so and we are here to inquire about our own paths as well." My heart stammers as I reply, nerves tumbling through me for a reason unknown to me. The witch turns their head to the side as if in thought, considering what should be revealed.

"You do not come for merely a glimpse into the coming tomorrows." A smile splits through their face showcasing glistening black teeth, pointed and dripping saliva. "Ask me for the knowledge you yearn to possess."

I didn't come with specific questions prepared, but witches know our thoughts more than we do at times. If the Ancient Vala is as ancient as claimed, they may know what no books, or witness accounts can answer. "Who is the Regent?"

"Who? I think you mean *what*." The word practically spits out of their mouth. "He is a crime to his power. Traipsing on soil not meant for his feet. Hungry for a chair when he could have a kingdom." Their words do little to ease my confusion, especially when he currently sits in my "*chair*" and yearns to steal my kingdom.

"How does he live for so long? He was an adult when he killed my great-grandparents, surely he should have turned to dust by now."

Their body begins to shake, a choking chortle coming from their chest and throat—are they laughing?

"The *magic* of fuel and betrayal flows through his veins, yet that is not how he continues to live. How does anything continue to live? I have seen a thousand years—the Gods have seen many more."

I sense that this is a question that will be left unanswered, although their own lifespan does give me something to ponder.

"There is much to come for you, Bree Ragna. You will part the poisoned clouds, fight amongst the dead, and claim a valor that shan't be seen. At least...not within your eyes." The raspy drawl fades with the last of their words. Words of my future, however cryptic they may be, send a chill down my spine.

"And for me?" Annie's voice shakes slightly as she asks.

"Annalysa–"

"Annie. Please, I'm just Annie."

"There is no, 'just Annie', in a fate like yours. Within days you will step from a shadow and rise. You will be an only heir, and yet another will remain in your company."

"What does that–"

"No. You do not question, only listen."

Annie is so taken back by the abruptness in the Vala's tone that I can hear the moment her jaw snaps shut and teeth clash together. The leather wrapped bones of the Vala's arms extend to both of us, spindly fingers reaching for what we owe. We each place locks of our hair tied with a ribbon in their outstretched hands, having prepared our gifts when Asa explained how these interactions work. Satisfied, the arms retreat, and Annie and I stand to make our exit.

"One more thing—a token of goodwill."

I turn back to face the skeletal being once more. Annie stays facing me—or most likely, the door—and gives me an agitated glance before focusing her stare to the ground. She is more than ready to leave the presence of the Vala.

"You know what is coming and you'd do well to prepare. Ragnarök waits for no one, not even the children of Gods."

TWENTY-SEVEN

BREE

Chaos engulfs the empty streets.

Curtains that blow in the summer winds along the shop windows are replaced with flames. Screams of crying children and mourning parents surround the soon to be ruins, coming from every building in the market. My lungs burn as hot as the town around me, my chest heaving in worry and a fierce determination.

The Regent has Annie, and his monsters are killing us all.

I run down the cobbled street, smoke consuming the air while my body pushes me further, the burning in my chest swells closer to combustion. These paths are unknown to me—the city unrecognizable.

The world weighs heavy for the cries of the living over the silence of the dead. A dread that consumes me from the inside out, similar to the screams that flood my head, urges me to run faster.

Faster.

Faster.

Find her.

Save her.

At the end of the street waits a single door. I have no inkling as to what it could lead to, but it's the only way forward. The only way closer to my Annie. Pushing through the wooden frame, I'm led straight into darkness. I fall freely, my hair thrashes through the wind, my limbs go limp, and for the first time in ages I can take a clear breath. I close my eyes and relish the moments of freedom from the chaos, the fear, the blinding grief that tears at my soul every fucking day. In the darkness I can pretend that this is all a dream. In the darkness I am safe. In the darkness, I can breathe. But something inside of me warns me to savor those breaths. Savor the way my lungs continue to expand peacefully with only a lingering flame that grips them.

"Open your eyes, my love."

Destrin's voice pries my eyes open, reluctant to leave their peaceful abyss. I only fall for half a second longer before I slam into a dry, sandy field. The world is no longer cast in black, but the sight before me is much, much darker.

I have landed in The Deadlands, the desert outside of Einherjor. The bodies of soldiers line the field, piled high in a grotesque organization of the dead. Some have been dead for only moments, and in others it is clear they have been dead for decades at least. Roaring from flames that rise incredible heights almost overpower the sounds of clashing swords nearby.

I run toward a hill straight ahead, searching for anything that will tell me where my daughter is. As I crest the top of the hill, I see the effects of our war with the Regent in full view. Throughout the vast empty space, warriors crash into each other. The living fight the dead, the dead fight the dead. Almost immediately I can see that the roaring is not from the flames taller than trees—I wish it were that simple.

Crushing humans below in its massive gait, Fenrir summons fire from his mouth and kills hundreds of warriors in one fell swoop of his flames. The giant wolf has been said to be chained nearby for over a millennia—chained with dwarf forged metal made from the sound of a cat's footfall, the beard of a woman, the roots of mountains, the sinews of the bear, the breath of a fish, and the spittle of birds. All things unknown to our realm, sacrificed to hold captive a son of none other than the trickster God of greed, Loki. His reckoning can only mean one thing.

Ragnarök is upon us.

It's then I realize I'm not on a hill, but a cliff. Below me lies the sea of the dead, a graveyard of fallen men due to die in the prophesied end of the world. Behind me lies the sea that all fear. The Haunted Sea has been said to be the place where Loki's other son, Jörmungandr holds the end of his tail in his mouth. The cries and wails that echo over the waters are reflections of his sorrow, betrayal, anger, and drive for revenge upon the God who put him there.

Sweeping my gaze across the land, I finally spot Annie. Tessa pulls her by the arm, urging her to run. Panic fuels my mother, pulling Annie away from the sea edge with all of the strength she can muster. Rising from the sea are the blackened scales of the serpent's head, and his piercing bloody eyes that follow. His deadly gaze has no other target but my family, so I run.

The second his mouth emerges from the water, he emits a poisonous cloud in a blood curdling hiss. I watch as my mother and daughter run as quickly as they can away from the omen of death, and they nearly make it to temporary safety.

No matter how fast I run; no matter how hard I push myself to reach them, my body doesn't move a single inch from my spot upon the cliff. I am forced to witness to the chaos as The Regent steps out from behind a long ruined building, separating Annie from my mother's grasp, and tossing her right into the path of the toxic cloud.

My body shoots up so quickly that I can practically feel my brain hit the inside of my skull. Sweat soaks through my clothes and into the thin mattress given by Asa and Zander. This was not a mere nightmare; I'm accustomed to those. My loved ones are harmed or killed in all of the nightmares, but Annie has always been safe. Right before something bad happens something always comes in to protect her, or show me that she's okay. But this time—this time I witnessed her demise. A poison that destroyed her, a sickening thud as she was thrown to the ground.

This was a dream sent as a message from the God's. This is the fate that I must change. Many will die in the battle of Ragnarök, but I will ensure that it's not *everyone* like the prophecy states–certainly not Annie.

I toss the sheets aside and head for the steam house. My body aches after the trip to and from the Vala's home, and I'm hoping the heat from the bath will sooth my body and my mind after the dream.

The warmth of the water engulfs my senses, finally allowing me to focus on one thought at a time. Although we have slightly veered off course, the whispers of the Vala will prove useful in the end, providing a small warning of what to expect.

Cryptic as they were.

Picturing Annie and my mother ensnared in Jörmungandr's path of poison makes the hair along my arms rise in a chill despite the heat of the room. The green fog stretches across the battlefield and just before I torture myself with the image of their peril, a clear path splits the cloud right down the middle. A raspy voice invades my thoughts, "*You will part the poisoned clouds, fight amongst the dead, and claim a valor that shan't be seen. At least...not within your eyes.*"

The entire way back to Asa and Zander's home I ran those words through my head over and over, hoping there is something I'm missing. Fear freezes the blood within me, unable to understand how I could possibly fight amongst the dead unless I turn into a draugr myself. It's not the fear of death that stills my heart—rather the fear of what would become of my daughter if I suffer such a fate.

But now...now there is hope. Given to me by the Gods through their message from the Vala. If I can save my family from the impossible, then I will gladly accept any fate destined for me.

With rejuvenated motivation, I finish my bath, and plan the next steps toward our goal. I will be sure to meet with the boys and Annie the moment the sun brightens the sky, for it's time to find our way to my dear Uncle.

TWENTY-EIGHT

ANNIE

Dreading the journey through any part of The Frostreik again—even if the ravens ensure the Jotungangr will not harm us—I take comfort in the hoard of pastries that Asa baked for our journey. When we hugged the couple goodbye, tears brimmed her soft eyes. Somewhere in the days they took care of us and we were welcomed into their home, a familial bond formed that I'll never forget.

Asa's tight hugs and warm words filled a gap in my heart, fueling the need inside of me to save my grandmother, wherever she may be. Will she have the same comforting warmth as Asa? Will she have the same smell of fresh cut wood and baked bread? After a bath, that is. Who knows what state she's in.

Amidst the sadness from leaving our new friends behind, resilience lingers as well. Gungnir is in our possession, glamoured to look like a dagger on my hip as to not make us a target for any hidden Regent cronies or creatures. Mother is confident that she has solved one piece of the Vala's puzzle, and my new found uncles have promised to travel with us as humans until the end, whatever the end may mean for us.

Having the two beings by our side, who have helped and saved us on multiple occasions thus far, has added a bounce to our gait as we shine with a confidence we didn't have before. I can appreciate the visit my mother insisted upon with the fire sprites in Gledibyr in more depth now, understanding that having powerful allies by our side makes this entire mission feel slightly less impossible.

BEST BY FAR

The days go by fairly quickly during the trip to Frostfjord. We decided to travel along the path that would lead us toward the Vala, straying slightly to the right as to evade their hut and bring us closer to the edge of The Frostreik. Thank the Gods for Zander with that idea, if I had to spend half a week in the tundra again I might lose my mind–and toes.

Tomorrow we'll finally arrive in the snowy, lakeside town where we'll rent a small boat for passage across The Great Lake to Drake's Port. As long as things have been going well on his end, Uncle Jaris should have begun checking Drake's Port for our arrival every couple of days by now. The hike up the Frostheim Mountains to reach Drake's Landing is treacherous—hardly anyone attempts it. It's said the locals of the city never risk the trek, but they have no reason to leave anyway. When I asked Mother how she expects us to get there, all she said was, "Uncle Jaris has his ways, and they are incredibly exciting. You won't be disappointed, but I refuse to ruin the surprise." Leaving me confused, as always.

We make camp once the sky begins to fade into a deep lilac. We only set up one of the tents we were given, but none of us use it. Each of us has our bedrolls set next to the campfire; sitting cross-legged, lounging with head in hands, laying down to read stories in the stars.

Camp is quiet, yet peaceful.

Salted jerky makes its way around our circle, an excuse for contact with each other while we wait for the morning light, apparently none of us welcome sleep. No breezes rustle the trees, but the air of the forest has a bone deep chill, all-consuming if not for the fire. Once we arrive in Drake's Landing, the real planning will begin—with real action. It's inevitable that there will be a battle, that much is clear.

Something about the night changes the energy in our group, where a few hours ago we held our chins high with confidence and excitement; we now burrow into our minds, attempting to hide from the uncertainty that now surrounds us.

The change was gradual; I hadn't noticed the tension in the air until the silence went from peaceful to uncomfortable. I look around the fire at each member of my family; Aeven and Elvind both stare into the flame, the space around their eyes tightened with their intense stares and down turned mouths. My mother stares into the sky, laying with her hands folded on her belly and her hair splayed around her face. What she sees in the stars, I can only guess, but in the reflection of the fire against her eyes I notice desperation and worry.

The weight of the world rests on my mother's shoulders, evident in the age that now cradles her eyes and the way the lines on her face deepen in thought constantly. She carries responsibility wherever she goes, trying to keep her shoulders straight and steady, but they inevitably slope as the days go on. I know she wants to save the world from Ragnarök and save our people from the usurper, but she wants to keep me alive and safe more than anything else. That is the worry that I see in her as she gazes mindlessly into the night sky.

Every plan she makes in our journey is not only centered around me, but everything that she has lost as well. I wish she could have experienced a long life with my father. I wish even more that I could have grown up without the fear of losing me tainting her every choice ever since his death.

In no way could I ever begrudge her for that. While anxiety laces her every movement over the years, so does love, compassion, and strength. Pa isn't here to remind her that she exists too, that she matters as much as any of us. So while she plots and plans the future of our Kingdom while keeping me in mind, I'll be there to ensure she has a place in the world as well.

Sleep does eventually weigh heavily upon me, and I tuck myself in to face the fire. Before drifting off I hear the soft snores from her across from me, and almost inaudible whispers from my uncles as they pace around the perimeter of our space. Before long I doze into my dreams, anxious to see what the Gods have in store for us in the morning.

The sun is bright, the snow approaches, and our funny feathered friends are nowhere to be found. I notice two cups of tea and pastries warm on a flat stone in the middle of the still-glowing remains of our fire. Mother hands one of the mugs before I can fully open my eyes, forcing me to sit up more quickly than I'd prefer first thing in the morning.

"Where have Aeven and Elvind gone?" I ask groggily, my throat thick with sleep.

"They said that they were being summoned by their steward, they'll meet us in Frostfjord." Her voice is monotone and her words are short—clearly not thrilled about them leaving.

"Well, I'm sure they will. They haven't broken a single promise yet. It's evident they want to be by our side."

She gives a tight nod in agreement and turns to continue packing up the few things scattered around camp. Her every movement is stiff and aggressive, so different from the way she lounged beside the fire last night. It's more than them just leaving, I realize, something else seems to be bothering her.

Before I have a chance to ask what's wrong, she continues to face the forest but stands with her back completely straight and quietly tells me, "I just can't shake the feeling that they're not going to be meeting us there. They seemed uncertain, uncomfortable even." She spins on her heels to meet my gaze, urging me with that single look to understand, "Something isn't right, but I don't think they're deceiving us. Whoever their steward is, they've never seemed very keen to speak of him."

"Did they ever mention where they hail from?"

"I believe somewhere near Frostfjord. We can stay an extra couple of days to give them a chance to show up. If not, we can ask Uncle Jaris if he has any information on a man of title with two wards." My mother speaks more to herself than me, like she is trying to convince herself to move forward no matter what. "Do you notice anything strange as well? Something similar to when those boys drowned years ago? I know you cannot control when they come to you but...I just need to be sure they're well." She doesn't add that the most recent "feeling" I had was when the draugr killed my father, but I suppose she's been haunted by his death enough recently.

I shake my head sadly while looking into my mug of tea. Her back slumps with disappointment that I cannot give her the answer she craves. Despite not being able to feel if something bad is going to happen, I don't want her to feel hopeless, but have nothing more to offer her besides, "It's good that I don't sense anything like that, isn't it? I choose to see the hope in that, and I hope you can too."

She moves around camp with less tension than before, allowing my words to resonate with her.

By the time she is finished packing up and we both finish our breakfast, the sun is almost in the middle of the sky. We never start our travels this late into the day, but I think my mother just wants to give the ravens as much time as possible to meet us later on.

The closer we get to the village, the heavier the snowfall is. Frostfjord is right at the end of The Frostreik, the gate back into civilization, so it adapts the same weather—unfortunately for me. As soon as I spot the bustling port and the shimmering water of The Great Lake, I release an exasperated sigh. We're so close to a warm bed and tasty meal that I'm practically drooling already. My mother chuckles quietly at my reaction to seeing the village, but I know she has to be just as relieved. For her this is another box to check on her journey list, we're so close to meeting Uncle Jaris that it's hard to ignore our growing excitement. Our pace picks up substantially and our first stop is the local pub that has rooms upstairs.

After we place out things in our shared room, Mother goes down to get us some food. Hopefully Aeven and Elvind return soon, having to add more loved ones to our growing list of people to find is the last thing we want to have to do. I flop onto my bed and a moan escapes my lips as soon as my skin touches the fur lined quilt. This is easily the softest blanket I've ever touched in my life. I crawl underneath and am immediately engulfed in a warmth usually only given by a roaring fire. Before I know it, I fall into a deeper sleep than I have in days.

I jerk awake when my mother opens the door sometime later, the fire in the hearth has shrunk significantly, telling me how long she has been gone for.

"Sorry honey, I got caught up downstairs. A man who works as a guide across the lake has offered his services to bring us over to Drake's Port in two days." A small smile graces her lips while her eyes have a renewed sparkle in them. She places a tray with our dinner—juicy chicken thighs with mashed potatoes and gravy—on the small table between our beds, sitting on hers excitedly before she continues. "This gives the boys plenty of time to get back to us, and enough time for us to rest. And it just so happens that the schedule Uncle and I made means that he should be looking for us there in two days as well."

Satisfied with how the day has gone so far, I sit back against my pillows and pull my plate of food onto my lap, allowing myself to appreciate the smells of the seasoning and gravy before digging in. Everything will work itself out, we'll soon be in the home of arguably our greatest ally, and can prepare for the war coming our way. Now, we just need Aeven and Elvind to meet us here.

TWENTY-NINE
BREE

They never came.

THIRTY

ANNIE

Two days have never felt so incredibly long until now.

Two days filled with anxiety over the safety of the boys.

Two days of growing silence between my mother and I.

Two days of questioning our entire journey up to this point.

The silence in our room these days has only been broken by the spit of the fire, my mother's pacing across the floorboards, and the occasional soft knock on the door from a woman my mother paid to bring us our meals.

Finally, during our last day and only a couple of hours before our agreed time to get to the docks, she speaks more than a few words to me, "Something isn't right. Even before, they were never too far from us for this long, we always spotted them in the sky and trees." Her voice is strong, albeit somber.

"What shall we do? We could stay another week, head to Drake's Port on the next day Uncle Jaris should be looking for us." I offer my solution lightly, not wanting to stay here any longer than we have to. Anyway, sitting here and waiting will do nothing to help us or the boys.

If we are going to find them then we need to leave here, reevaluate our path. Do we go to Uncle Jaris for help first? Do we try to listen to gossiping villagers around here who might know of their steward? Is there even a way that we can help without completely compromising everything that we have done so far? Doubt attacks my mind, how can we save our kingdom when we have yet to save a single member of our family. Plus, do they even need to be saved?

"As much as I'd love that, I fear it would just waste time. We already have no inkling of the amount of time we have left, we cannot continue to wait here when we need to keep going." It sounds more like she is trying to convince herself more than anything else, but I nod in agreement, relieved that we'll leave today as planned, despite my worries.

Packing our things only takes a few moments, only a change of clothes was needed from our packs while we had our travel worn ones washed last night. We have our breakfast at the bar and I'm grateful for the social interactions. Not having any distractions while we waited in our room made the time feel like weeks rather than days, but mother insisted we stay hidden.

Being closer than ever to Valderra has us both on edge, anyone working for The Regent could easily find their way to Frostfjord for a drink. This is where diplomatic meetings between Drake's Landing and the other cities take place, as it's too difficult to travel through the Frostheim mountains where the city is perched. And with Uncle Jaris playing his part as faithful to the Regent, those men would be welcomed here. Besides Valderra, we're also closer to Skalborg than before—triggering my mother more than ever.

"Why are you so afraid of the Jarl of Skalborg?" I whisper.

Her shoulders tighten, and she grips her mug of tea tightly with both hands, lips pursed and nostrils flaring. "*He* is there. My step father. Tessa wanted to forget him, pretend he never existed after they separated—not me. As I grew older I would ask Uncle Jaris in letters to help me keep watch of his movements. It turns out, he's one of The Regent's most trusted men–inner circle with Jaris. If he spots me, this is all over."

A shiver runs through me. I knew she was worried about the Jarl, I had no idea it went as deep as him being the source of her childhood trauma. She finishes her tea and sets the mug onto the bar a little more abruptly than I think she meant, so I put my hand over hers in support. I receive a small smile in return, and she turns to pay the barmaid for our meal.

We gather our packs from beside us and I ensure the spear's glamour is still intact and attached to the hidden holster on my hip. I pull my tunic and cloak over to conceal it, and we make our way outside toward The Great Lake.

Bards have written many songs about this lake. Being the largest body of water on the continent and the most accessible way to Drake's Port make it incredibly popular. They sing of its beauty, the way the waves sparkle under the sun like a gentle snowfall, how the water is as clear as the sky on a bright summer's day. Others sing of the monsters rumored to live in its depths, large scaly creatures that poke their heads up to watch incoming boats drift past. Some claim to have even seen Jörmundgandr himself here, though the Serpent Sound between Skogby and home is named after the legendary snake and more commonly rumored to be his home.

Freshly frozen snow crunches beneath our feet as we wind through the village streets to find the boathouse. The place is quaint, busy for the locals but not an overwhelming fury of people bustling through. The houses and shops are smaller than what I'm used to seeing, completely dwarfed by the sheer magnitude of the Diplomatic building. Even the boathouse is larger than most of the homes.

Aged planks of wood make up the structure of the building and the roof bows inward, either from the age of the wood or from years of constant snow. Once inside, my jaw hits the floor. Lining each wall are canoes of all sizes, suspended in the air by thick ropes and iron pulleys. They even hang from the rafters, forming my new theory for the bowed roof.

My mother approaches a desk positioned against the back wall where a young man sits with his legs crossed on the surface, whittling what looks to be a small duck. Once he notices us, he quickly lowers his legs, almost falling out of the stool. He plasters on his best smile, which I'm sure is reserved specifically for customers, and wishes us a good morning.

"How can I help ya, ladies?" He sounds as friendly as can be, but my heart sinks when he doesn't register that this was a planned meeting.

"Hello, I met a man at the inn the other night, he told me he would give us passage across the lake today. I believe he said his name was Bo?" She looks around the space, presumably for any sign of the man.

"Aye, Bo mentioned that. Sad to say that he and his ol' lady caught the bug, he won't be in for who knows 'ow long. My mate can bring ya though! I'll grab him." The young man jumps off the stool and runs through a door I didn't notice, yelling the name Ivar as he goes. Within a minute he returns with a burly dark haired man close behind. The moment he catches my mother's eye, he stops in his tracks and looks in awe. He adjusts himself just as quickly, forcing his sight back on the desk.

My mother evidently notices this and confronts him. "I'm sorry, sir. Have we met before?" Her tone is polite and firm, eyes holding him captive—a command.

"No." He responds without hesitation.

The silence following takes control of the atmosphere, causing us all to glance awkwardly at one another. The friendly man pretends to shuffle some papers around, and I can't help but lean from one foot to the other waiting for someone to say something. My mother, unbothered by his rudeness, stands tall with one eyebrow raised and her hands closed together gracefully in front of her, watching Ivar. Ultimately, he decides to amend his answer, "You look like someone I know, is all. Arne, what do you need?"

Satisfied with that, Arne cowers under the man's hulking frame since he looks so far over him that his long braided beard almost hits Arne in the face. He motions toward an open journal laid out in front of him where notes are written in a scrawl similar to chicken scratch. Apparently it makes sense to them both, because the man nods with a grunt and looks back at my mother and I. He tightens the tie that holds his waist length hair back and walks out of the entryway.

"Ladies, if you'd follow Ivar, please. He will bring ya where ya need to go." Arne sits back in his stool with his hands folded on the desk and gives us a sincere smile as we thank him and I follow my mother out the door to where she follows Ivar leisurely, not allowing him to rush her.

Once outside, we spot him untying the ropes that keep a large canoe tethered to the docks just down a small hill. Panic deep within my chest surges through me, settling and blooming along my spine, and limbs. Terror. Unyielding, unruly terror, just as my mother wished me to see. She's in danger, but I can't sense why. Are the rumors of monsters in the lake true? Will trouble be waiting for us at Port? I pull on her cloak like I did as a child to slow her down.

"Something doesn't feel right; you're in danger. I can't—I don't know why." I can't articulate what I am feeling, my words don't even sound like my own, they remind me of a child waking from a nightmare, small and unsure.

"Do you think it's the lake?" she asks hesitantly.

"I have no idea, with my father there was a clear enemy."

"Do you remember when your friends were taken by the sea, little one? You had a similar feeling. Your father and I were unharmed, simply shaken." She places her hands on my shoulders while attempting to comfort me, but to no avail. I remember the sheer panic I felt when they were readying to leave, but had no idea why. I knew something horrible would happen, but was too young to be able to see all of the different dangers that could threaten lives on such a happy island village. My cries for Samuel haunt me still, slipping into my dreams every now and then. I shake away the memory, I don't want it to stay with me today.

"Yes but–" Does she not remember how this led directly to the attack on our village? I need her to understand me at this moment. I can't find the words but I need her to know. My heart pounds in my chest, slamming into my bones, causing all of my blood to rush through me in panic—my head begins to spin. The edges of my vision threaten to darken, my limbs feel numb in my terror, and my chest *hurts* with the slamming and tightening of my heart.

She is in danger, and I will make her understand that.

I propel my magic from myself into her through our physical contact. Her body stiffens as she experiences briefly what I do and inhales a quick gasp. Her gaze is unfocused as she tries to manipulate the magic into a finite answer to the danger. Her face reddens in the attempt, but with a spastic few breaths and a hand to her chest, I know that it didn't work.

"Well, Annie, that was quite the experience. I've never tried projecting my emotions onto another before, that was…very intriguing to say the least." She continues trying to catch her breath, the intrigue she mentioned clear in her features.

Frustration with myself and anger at her floods through me, she's so focused on the magic I performed rather than the clear danger to her. She catches the heat in my cheeks and tries to reassure me before I can come up with a retort, "Honey, I hear you. I do. But we *have* to keep going. I will be more alert and ready to defend myself when the need arises."

Tears threaten to drown my sight, my thoughts consumed with love, irritation, and fear for my mother. She loops her arm through mine and takes us down the path where Ivar waits at the end in the boat. "Annie, if there was nothing to pose any danger to me then this journey would be over already, in fact, it would have never been necessary." She gives my arm a loving squeeze, I can feel her looking at me while I keep looking straight ahead. "In times like this, we cannot afford to turn tail and run when danger is near. We'll face whatever comes with full steam and vigor. We are Ragna's, after all. We are just built better." My fathers frequent words echo between us, calming me slowly. He would be just as resilient as her if he were here, confident that we can face any obstacle that comes our way because of who we are. His memory makes breathing come more easily. My chest is still tight, but the pounding slows.

Ivar grunts as we approach. Though his verbal manners are lacking, he still holds a calloused hand out to each of us as we take turns climbing in. We can spot the clearing of trees across the lake where our destination awaits, although it appears miniscule from this distance. The sky is gray but clear of heavy clouds.

Instead, thin dark wisps streak the sky, blocking the sun from shining through completely. They are not thick enough to threaten us with rain, but promise a dreary day. All I can think as we try to situate ourselves on the small bench-like seats is that I hope the weather is nice enough that we won't have to worry about strong tides.

Ivar pushes off against the dock with his massive foot, rocking the boat enough that I give a small yelp, making the man smile for the first time since we met him. He seems like the kind of man that would find someone's pain funny, not just laughing at someone because they were spooked.

The canoe glides through the water effortlessly, like it is simply floating through the sky. Being on the water is eerie in a way; I can still hear the hustle and bustle from Frostfjord, but it sounds more like an echo of civilization. The most prominent noise is the water as it circles around the oars when Ivar rows them under the surface, and the cascading drops sliding off of the wood when it breaks through the surface again.

My mother sits forward with her back straight and hands folded in her lap. She allows her gaze to wander across the span of the lake, but otherwise stays completely still. I envy her ability to do so because my nerves threaten to return only half an hour into the trip, my heart speeding its pace, but not yet pounding like before. I can't help but pick at the skin around my fingers and tap my foot silently against the inside of the boat.

The next two hours are painfully similar. No noises other than the movement of water, no laughter, and *especially* no small talk. The eerie quiet between us helps me sort through my racing thoughts, and scan the water around us for any potential threats—a welcome distraction.

When we finally near the docks at Drake's Port, Ivar decides to show his hand. He steals glances at the two of us, looking away quickly if we notice. Once we hear the magnified voices from land, he twists his neck at an absurd angle to search for something—someone, perhaps? I feel a nudge on the outside of my thigh and notice that my mother is hiding her movements, she doesn't want Ivar to see what she's doing.

Without looking, I take what is in her hand—a folded piece of parchment—and grip it tightly in my fist. Ivar doesn't notice our exchange, too preoccupied by whoever he's looking for nearby. Once we are a boat's length away from the dock he does a double take at a thin man on shore with a thick blonde mustache and large straw hat. He gives the man a nod and then faces us once more, brimming with confidence. The man walks down the dock and meets us as Ivar begins tying up the canoe, holding out a hand for me to take.

"What a beautiful day, is it not?" The wind blows short strands of dusty blonde hair from behind his ear, flapping wildly as they are trapped beneath his hat.

A newfound weariness shivers down my spine and I look to my mother for reassurance. Her eyes flash with a warning when they meet mine, but she gives a curt nod and refocuses on Ivar. When I safely disembark, he keeps a tight hold on my arm with an insincere smile plastered onto his weathered tan face. Before I can shrug him off, cold metal kisses the inside of my wrist—a hidden threat so as not to bring attention to us.

Ivar has my mother in a similar hold, still on the boat. I can feel his hot breath disturb the hair behind my ear as he whispers loud enough for my mother to hear as well. "Do not try to escape or I will bleed you dry right in these streets. Do you understand?"

I nod frantically, giving him the sense that I'm a weak, fearful girl. My mother does no such thing, she stares daggers into my captor's cold black eyes, daring him to even try to harm me.

The boat we were in sways back and forth with the waves, hitting the dock repeatedly. Crisp winds blow, tangle our hair and they tie our hands with rope and drag us down the docks and toward a covered wagon with two horses strapped to the front. We can't allow ourselves to be put inside, there may not be a chance to escape once trapped. Few people are in the area, making my hope for outside help tarnish. The few who *are* out and about stick to the shoveled pathways that lead from one small building to another, focused on their steps so as not to slip on the icy paths.

I try to get a read on Mother–to see if she has a plan brewing, but I'm met with nothing. Her face has gone completely still, it could convince a child she's made of stone. She makes no attempt to meet my gaze and continues to stare straight ahead. Soon her stormy mask will crack and we'll be free, my mother executing this escape with flair. Won't we?

With every second the wagon gets closer and closer, my confusion blends with panic, but I push the feelings down in order to focus–preparing to be of use when she needs me.

Ivar throws my mother over his shoulder like a sack of potatoes and places her on the ledge of the wagon, pushing her inside and looping the rope that binds her wrists onto a hook attached to the wall inside. Her toes just barely touch the floor, stretching her back as she tries not to let her shoulders hold all of her weight. Canvas flaps fall from the top, hiding her from my sight and from the rest of the world. Ivar adjusts the canvas as he begins to tease the man behind me, "Need some help with the lass, Sig?"

He growls in my ear, his horrid, hot breath choking me before responding. "I've got it handled. Get the horses ready." Ivar chuckles deeply and spins on his heel, striding to the front of the wagon.

My captor is not nearly as big or strong as him, he pulls out a collapsible wooden stool for me to walk up into the wagon rather than man-handling me. He climbs close behind me, allowing no space between us. As soon as my face breaks through the cover I spot my mother swinging by her wrists from side to side, bending and extending her knees to gain momentum.

"Down!" she yells.

As soon as I duck, Sig forces his head in behind me and is met with a swift kick to the nose. He's thrown backward off of the wagon with a sickening thud as he hits the icy road. "Run, Annie!" she continues, and I feel as if I have been struck as well.

"But...you..." I stumble over my words, she can't be serious. I can't just *leave* her–

"GO, NOW!" Tears spill down her cheeks—in fear for herself? For me?

I hesitate for a second more, feeling the wagon teeter to the side as Ivar grunts while jumping off the wagon to see what the commotion is about. As soon as he spots his accomplice's limp hand on the ground, he runs back to grab the horse's reins and starts forward—better to have one princess secured than none.

"I love you. I'll find you." I whisper to her.

She nods and attempts to smile, trying to reassure me as always. Before I can convince myself otherwise, I jump off the back of the wagon and hit the frozen ground with a roll. I use my wrists to lessen the impact and straighten myself out, but regret it immediately when a sharp crack pierces my ears. Pain shoots through my arms, but a feeling much worse batters my heart as I watch the wagon pull away with my entire world trapped inside.

EPILOGUE

BREE

A steady drip crashes against stone and echoes in my tomb. My body is frozen, I can barely move, let alone feel my stiffened limbs. I lay limp on a wet, uneven slab of stone. Occasionally the rattle of thick chains join the chorus of dripping water. Even more rare are the footsteps that bring a moldy loaf of bread and a cup I'm allowed to fill with the aforementioned source of dripping. Days go by like this, or is it weeks? Hours? Surely I would have withered away by now if it was any longer than a few days.

Any attempt I have made to reach my magic has failed. What normally feels like a pool of power within me has been completely dried up, not a drop to spare. The missing piece of me drains my resolve. Oh, what I would give to have Mead snuggled up against me for some even the smallest semblance of comfort, even if I could use magic for nothing else.

I tried convincing myself to eat more than just a couple of bites, but can hardly stomach it. So I continue to lay in this cold, dead prison cell, praying that Annie made it to my Uncle safely. The moment I realized what Ivar was doing, I knew I needed to give Annie the information necessary to access Uncle Jaris. The barmaid for the inn we were to meet at would have asked her for proof of her meeting; this is where she would have shown the slip of parchment with my Uncle's written permission I gave her for access. Without it, she would be denied.

Alone.

Waiting to be captured like me.

Her and Uncle have never met and don't know what the other looks like, trying to spot him going in or out of the inn would be tedious and dangerous if caught by anyone but him.

After the torturous wagon ride where my shoulders were surely mere moments from being torn from my body, I was blindfolded and thrown into this cell to await the company of whoever is behind this kidnapping.

Finally, it seems like my curiosity will be rewarded with answers when sharp echoes from a heeled shoe travel throughout the dungeon. Only a man of power would wear such footwear, I steel myself so that I show no weakness. My face floods with heat at this man's arrogance, walking through a dingy dungeon to do what, wave his privilege in my face?

Once the steps are so close that I could reach out and touch them in the pitch black, I hear the heavy dragging sound that accompanies them. The rusted cell door across from mine screeches in protest as it's opened and the dragging goes inside. With another ear-splitting noise of defiance the barred iron door closes, and the footsteps pause in front of my door.

A worn chuckle chases away any warmth I had left in my veins. The baritone stretches my ears open, ensuring I can hear nothing but him. I know this sound. It used to haunt my dreams and poison my childhood. Thriving in my fear, personally directing the performance he turned into my nightmares. He orders someone to light the sconces on either side of my cell, exaggerated shadows dance over his sharp features, pointed, mouse colored goatee and icy eyes. He adorns a red satin cloak with the collar straight against his neck. His shoes match the expensive fabric, screaming of his wealth–professing his *loyalty*.

"So good to see you again, Bree." My name on his tongue forces bile into my throat. I thought I was free of him. I thought I would never need to face him again. I would face the World Serpent with gratitude if it meant I would be away from the man before me. My throat is too dry to properly form words, so I do the only thing fitting in my current state.

I allow the bile to leave my throat, burning as it does, and aim right for his fancy heeled feet, just inches from my head.

With a curse and harsh kick to the bars of my cell, he rages—just as he always has. So easy to anger, it has always made me wonder what he must compensate for; being such a hateful man for no reason at all.

A soft whimper can be heard from the cell so recently opened and this stops him in his tracks. An eerie calm washes over him, something that has always stricken fear in my heart. I would take his malice over her calm on any occasion. Before me stands an entirely different persona than what I was witnessing just a breath ago. The thin split of his mouth widens over his sunken cheeks, emanating the very essence of mischief and evil. He clears his throat and smooths out the front of his cloak, gathering his composure. He twists his heels so that his entire body faces my direction and I'm forced to crane my neck as far as it will go to meet his disgusting, delighted stare.

"I'm so glad you could join us after all this time. You know what they say, families should never be apart forever. It seems you have finally come to your senses." Without any further explanation, he turns on his heels once more and swiftly leaves the dungeon.

For the first time during my imprisonment I'm able to see my surroundings, as he left the sconces lit before leaving. The incessant drip is feet away from the cup meant to be catching it. My bread has become more mold than food. My cell is big enough to fit a large family. Another prisoner mirrors my position in the cell parallel to mine.

A woman lays in a large puddle in the middle of her cell. Chocolate colored hair is dull and matted around her face. Her cheekbones yearn to break free from her paper thin skin, and her eyes are surrounded by purple pools of exhaustion. Long, thin fingers stretch toward nothing as they lay motionless on the ground. Her face is so pale, there would be no telling where her lips begin if it weren't for the bleeding cracks that line them. She is so thin under her ragged dress that I can't even get a sense of where her legs are, no hips or hills rise from the cloth. If she hadn't made that noise moments ago I'd be convinced she was dead. Her fearful whimper is what courses through my head now, replaying over and over until I remember that I have heard that noise before. For years, in fact.

For years I thought I was abandoned.

For years I would rage from the sheer audacity of her negligence.

For years she has laid here, chained in this prison.

For years she has been tangled and tortured in his web.

Bane's web.

A web we escaped so long ago, that it has since been reinforced and trapped her anew.

For years...her estranged husband has had her in his clutches for *years*.

Now he has me too.

ACKNOWLEDGEMENTS

I can't believe that the beginning story is finally in print. And it wouldn't have happened without a handful of people. So, without further adieu, I'd love to give thanks to my friends and family that have helped get this project going.

First, my daughter, Arwen. Without you, there would simply be no story. Becoming a mother has changed me in a hundred ways, and inspired me in a thousand more.

Then, there are the friends who have pushed, encouraged, and believed in me enough to fulfill this dream of mine. If you don't have an Amber, Jana, or Fern in your life then I suggest you fix that. I'm so grateful to have friends like you three, and I absolutely would not have reached this step without you guys. Watching you all work so hard to complete your own books and dreams has been more of an inspiration than you know.

I'd also love to say thank you to my mans, Dustin. I never knew that I could feel so safe and secure with a person until I met you. Destrin wouldn't be half the character he is without you to be such an inspiration. Thank you for being such a wonderful human being & the father a little girl should never go without. You heal so much more within me than you know <3

Lastly, thank you to all of the incredible friends I have made via Instagram. I never thought I could make such powerful connections over the internet, and then all of you came barreling in to my life. What started as me just posting about books I've read & loved, has turned into me accomplishing goals I never thought possible for myself. You have all done so much for me with your support and love, thank you.

There are many others who fall under the, "I'm grateful for you " umbrella, but there is another book coming, so you will have your time to shine.

P.S. Skye, you're fired.

ABOUT THE AUTHOR

In a hole in the ground there lives Brittany. Not a nasty, dirty, wet hole, but it is close. In a den made of books and empty coffee mugs lives Brittany and her merry petting zoo. Between five house cats, a rabbit, and a chinchilla, this wanna-be hobbit and her family are kept quite busy. After toddler snuggles and watching videos her husband finds absolutely necessary to show her, she finds time to write her books and more importantly, read others.

Somewhere between wanting to be a surgeon and a marine biologist when she grew up, Brittany also wanted to be an author. Always being more of a reader than a writer, but loving English class, this seemed like a goal that was *slightly* out of reach—until now.

Follow Brittany on Instagram @bea.rose.books to stay informed on future projects & the occasional gushing over a book she read. You can also go to her website for more info: www.brittanygravesbooks.com

Made in the USA
Columbia, SC
05 April 2025